ABOUT THIS BOOK

The story of Mavis and Cameron's romance and fight to be together continues in this sequel to *Plans Laid Bare*.

With the fear of discovery by her evil grandfather behind her and her demonic power growing stronger every day, Mavis LeGrand is content in the mountains of Colorado. Her incubus fiancé, Cameron, loves her, and things seem to be going as well as can be expected, but she knows behind the picturesque town and smiling faces, an evil lurks, just waiting for her to let her guard down long enough to snatch away the peace she's found.

Determined to push through her growing unease, Mavis throws herself into finding a way to get Cameron's soul back from her soon-to-be father-in-law. At the same time, she's dealing with the incubus's insatiable desires and the budding romance between her best friend and the ridiculously unsuitable demon who's crashing in their spare bedroom.

With a strong feeling of malice lingering over the town like a dense fog, Mavis can sense that she'll soon be in for a fight, albeit a battle she knows she can win. Evil has no place in Havenwood Falls, and she'll be damned if she lets anyone or anything hurt the town or the ones she loves.

HAVENWOOD FALLS SIN & SILK BOOKS

Taming the Beast by Nadirah Foxx

Plans Laid Bare by JD Nelson

Shift of Fate by Victoria Escobar

Stolen Wishes by Victoria Flynn

Damned Allure by Justine Winter

Savage Salvation by Kristie Cook

Dark Seduction by Michele G. Miller & R.K. Ryals

Soul Laid Bare by JD Nelson

Stray With Me by E.J. Fechenda

Chase the Flames by Desiree Lafawn

Flirting With Death by Nadirah Foxx

Also try the signature line, Havenwood Falls, the historical paranormal line, Legends of Havenwood Falls, and stories from the local supernatural college in Sun & Moon Academy.

Stay up to date at www.HavenwoodFalls.com

ALSO BY J.D. NELSON

Wicked Ways Series

A Night of Wickedness

All I Want For Christmas Are My Two Front Fangs: A Wicked Ways Companion Novel

Wolves Will Be Wolves

Too Cute To Spook: A Wicked Ways Companion Novel

Night Aberrations Series

Night Aberrations

The Fire within the Night

Stand Alone Novels

Control: A Tale of Desire

SOUL LAID BARE

A HAVENWOOD FALLS SIN & SILK NOVELLA

J.D. NELSON

To Nels, always Nels

CHAPTER 1

*A*s I filled out my billionth online job application for the month, I lamented the fact that I couldn't add *demon-killing badass* to my list of job skills. I mean, what's the use of having a kick-ass power like that if you couldn't use it to pad a skimpy résumé? Sure, accounting had fascinated me in my pre–Exitium Daemonium days, but now, it bored me to tears. These days, I needed a job that had a bit of excitement and room to be promoted, not a dull stay-at-home position where my best coworker friend was a calculator.

"Ugh," I said, sighing as I stood up from Cameron's desk and stretched. "I'm officially sick of the job hunt. I think I'm going to take a page out of your book and become an escort."

"What was that, darling?" asked a deep voice gruff with sleep.

"Nothing," I told my fiancé, ogling his muscled chest and the erection lifting the sheet as I climbed onto our king-sized bed to join him. "Well, nothing unless you like dull employment that makes you want to tear your hair out by the roots."

He flashed the devilish grin he knew made me weak in the

knees and stroked my hair back from my forehead. "How could I like anything that changes one strand of your beautiful blond hair?"

"So," I said, straddling his hips and leaning in for a kiss. "You think my hair is beautiful?"

Cameron tugged me tight against his erection, a smoldering look of desire in his honey-brown eyes. "I think every part of you is beautiful, Mavis, no matter what color your hair."

I closed my eyes and let my body gradually change from a blond-haired, blue-eyed young woman to the pale demon with white-blond hair and silver eyes he preferred. "Better?"

He grinned and lifted my shirt over my head, taking care not to catch it on the tiny twin horns above my hairline. "As soon as I get you naked, it will be."

"I think I can make that happen," I told him, giggling as he shivered from the chill of my partially ice-covered skin.

A loud bang sounded against the wall we shared with our neighbor, making us both jump. Cam groaned and glared at the wall. "For the love of everything holy."

I suppressed another giggle. "I guess Penelope is awake . . . and still in her sex drought."

"I'm willing to ignore her if you are," he said, thumbing my hardened nipples through my bra.

I rocked against him, lost in the sensation, and gasped out, "You know she won't stop," when he fell into rhythm with me.

He sighed and flopped back onto his pillow, giving up. "Fine, but if she doesn't let us have some very enthusiastic sex in my own bed soon, we're moving to Tibet."

I laughed at his cynicism, but on this one, I was in perfect agreement with him. She had interrupted us so many times in the last week, I was thinking about talking to the management about permanent soundproofing or maybe even eviction.

But to be entirely fair, our mutual bestie wasn't exactly keeping us completely celibate. Because of Cam's nearly insatiable incubus appetite, we were still having sex two or three times a day. We just weren't allowed to have sex within earshot of our not-by-choice-chaste neighbor.

To be honest, I didn't care where we had it as long as we had it. Cam's father might have taken his humanity when he'd taken his soul, but he was still the same tall, dark, and inappropriate guy I'd met on the side of the road five months ago while I was on the run from my own crazed family member. In almost every single way, he hadn't changed one bit. He still made me laugh with his charming, sarcastic wit, and, of course, he was still the sexed-up asshole I wanted to smack upside the back of his head on occasion.

All in all, I couldn't complain too much. Things were pretty close to perfect in the little life we'd carved out in Havenwood Falls —apart from Cam's stolen soul; the looming threat of my future father-in-law, Severin DeSalle, trying to kidnap me to use my demon-killing power for his own evil purposes; my jobless state; and a neighbor actively trying to keep me from getting laid, that is.

Okay, so maybe things weren't that great. But we had to play the hand we were dealt, right?

Penelope knocked on my front door mere seconds after she heard Cam reluctantly leave to meet his latest client. Brunette and bubbly, the brown-eyed beauty usually had a happy expression pasted on her face, but what stood in front of me on this day was a downtrodden, hopeless wreck.

"What's wrong?" I asked, pulling her inside to keep the heat from escaping. Ice demon or not, I wasn't immune to Colorado's frigid temperatures, and Penelope was an expert at complaining about my cold apartment . . . or really anything that was pissing her off.

"It's Ray," she said, sighing as she shed her bright red coat.

"Nooooo," I whined. "No more demon problems, Penny. I have enough demon problems of my own, you know."

She frowned. "That six-month deadline Severin implemented is coming up pretty quickly, isn't it?"

"Very," I muttered, taking the coat from her and hanging it on a hook near the door. "But it's not as if I'm actually going to let him use me or my powers for his plot for world domination or whatever he's up to."

Brows raised, she asked, "Oh, have you and Cam finally come up with a plan to stop him?"

"No. Well, sort of. Do you think sticking my size sixes up his ass will work?"

"I don't know," she said, smirking. "He's an incubus. He might actually like that."

I glared at her. "I'm telling Cam you said that."

She glared back. "Fine."

"And then I'm telling Ray you want to have his demon baby," I added for good measure.

Penelope looked off into the distance and shrugged.

"Penny, no."

She threw her hands up, exasperated. "Well, what do you expect? The constant innuendo is slowly wearing me down. Realistically, I don't know how much longer I can resist him."

My jaw dropped. "He's actually wearing you down with those terrible sex jokes and thinly veiled come-ons?" I shook my head. "You know, I think that might say more about you than him."

"Yes! And screw you!" she exclaimed, throwing herself into the corner chair. "Do you know how hard it is to turn down sex from a hot demon like Ray?"

I stared at her. "Are you seriously asking me that question right now?"

She laughed, remembering her interference in my super-sexy-happy-fun-time this morning. "Oh, yeah. I guess you do."

"Of course I do! You won't let me have mind-blowing sex with my freakin' fiancé in my own bed, you jealous cow!"

Penelope threw her hands up. "Do you think I want to stop you?"

I raised an eyebrow.

"Okay, maybe I do, but fuck, Mavis, I can't take hearing the constant banging anymore. I'm about to start humping the furniture over there!"

I wrinkled my nose. "Gross. Stay away from the couch. We just managed to get that spot of disintegrated evil henchman out of it."

"Ew."

"No more 'ew' than you lusting after Rayonus," I said.

"He's Ray," she deadpanned.

She had a point there. Rayonus Rixa, or Ray as we called him in secret, was smoking hot. He was tall and dark-haired with a creepy bright blue and solid black eye combo that would give any normal woman nightmares, but he was also every bit the devious, troublemaking demon your mother warned you about. He had a knack for always being there with a bad idea or to influence you into doing something you'd normally never do. For Penelope, he was her sexual kryptonite. For me, he was a good demon friend of Cam's that had been squatting in our guest bedroom for the past four months.

Penelope sighed. "I don't know how much more sexual tension I can take before I crack, Mavis. Every time he stares me down with that black demon eye of his, I need a fresh pair of panties. Why is that so fucking hot?"

"What's this about needing new panties?" Ray asked, opening the front door and stomping the snow off his boots.

"You could knock, you know," I griped.

A smile spread across his disturbingly handsome face as he said, "I could, indeed, Miss LeGrand, but then I wouldn't hear half of the dirty things that come out of Penny's mouth." Then he hung his coat next to Penelope's and traipsed into the kitchen like he didn't have a care in the world.

I rolled my eyes. If anything, Ray was consistent with the effortless charm and bullshit.

When he was out of hearing distance, I sat on the arm of Penelope's chair and leaned over to ask, "Have you considered just getting it over with? It's clear both of you want to fuck each other's brains out."

"He's a demon," she said, as if that settled it.

"Um, I'm a demon," I countered.

"Yeah, but you're a good demon, and you're not trying to fuck me."

"True, but you don't know that Ray isn't decent deep, deep, deep down."

She lifted an eyebrow. "I don't?"

"Okay, he's probably not," I conceded. "But a little demon dick won't kill you, Penelope. Ray can't take your soul like Cam can."

"I don't need a little demon dick!" Penelope hissed.

"That's good to hear," Ray said, coming out of the kitchen with a glass of water. "Because I've got more than you can handle, Penny."

"Stop calling me Penny!" she snapped at him.

He inclined his head, a small smile playing on his lips. "As you wish, Miss Osbourne."

Penelope and I rolled our eyes and went back to ignoring him.

"I was thinking about going to Callie's," I said, changing the subject. "Do you want to tag along after work tomorrow? I remember you saying you needed a skirt to go with that white eyelet top."

Before Penelope could answer, Ray said, "A skirt is a fantastic idea, Penny. I do love easy access."

"Don't you have somewhere to be?" I asked, annoyed. "And

before you answer, remember that I can destroy you where you stand."

The sarcastic smile he wore fell from his lips. "You know, I do think I have an appointment elsewhere. I believe I'll bid you beautiful ladies adieu for the afternoon."

Penelope watched him quickly retreat with a wistful expression. "He's going to my apartment, isn't he?"

"You're the one who showed him where you keep the spare key," I pointed out, shaking my head. "Honestly, I don't know why you're putting off the inevitable. Fuck him or don't fuck him—I don't care —but you have to do something soon. This can't go on forever. Cameron is starting to get really pissed with the blue-ball situation you're forcing on him."

She groaned and buried her face in a beaded throw pillow. "I'm doomed."

"Doomed is better than damned around here these days," I reminded her, shrugging.

She lifted her head and narrowed her eyes at me. "I think Cam and Ray are starting to be a really shitty influence on you."

CHAPTER 2

*T*he next day, I met a peeved but much calmer Penelope outside of Callie's Consignments. The clothing and accessory store was usually bristling with activity, but today, it only had a handful of shoppers, a rarity to be sure. I, for one, was overjoyed. My bestie was a lot of things, but she wasn't quiet. She didn't seem to have a volume button when it came to conversing about my love life, or really any topic, in public.

And today would be no different. I could tell she was already in a fine froth when she stomped toward the store, looking cuter than anyone should be allowed to look in her restaurant uniform and fur-lined parka. Something had set her off—something big.

"People are schmucky jerkwads," she informed me, kissing my cheek.

"Agreed," I said. "Want to talk about it?"

"No, let's just spend Cam's money."

I laughed. "Oh, is Cam floating this little outing?"

"Fuck yeah, he is. He promised he would do anything to repay me for the awkwardness of last month's failed soul stealing, remember? I've decided that's going to be with actual money."

I winced as I remembered the unbearably long six seconds it took Cam to remember that his incubus seduction skills didn't work on Penelope (or anyone in Havenwood Falls) and the resulting mortification of him (a) doing it only one day after him proposing and putting a diamond the size of a brick on my finger and (b) trying to come on to his longtime best friend. He still didn't want to talk about what he'd dubbed "the incident," even in private.

Shuddering, I opened the door and said, "Rock on, sister. We are all ready to put that weirdness behind us."

She held her hands out as if Cam was still standing in front of her. "Yeah, but his face when he realized what he was doing will forever be etched into my memories. Shit, it's easily going to stay in the top ten. It. Was. Hilarious."

"I still can't think about it without laughing," I said, making the horrified yet disgusted face he'd made when he came out of whatever sex-seeking trance he was in that night.

We both burst into raucous laughter, then immediately stifled it when we got reproachful glares from the other patrons.

"Don't do that, Mavis! You're going to get us kicked out of here," Penelope reprimanded. "I still need to see if they have that aqua skirt from the window in my size."

"Fine," I said brightly. "We can talk about your date last night."

She shook her head, not looking me in the eye. "No. We really can't."

I turned to her with a pouty face. "Come on, Penny!"

"No. And it wasn't a date," she added glumly. "It was Ray, sitting on my couch, doing his best to get in my panties without actually touching them."

I stopped, unwilling to go farther down the aisle until she gave me something. "What do you mean it wasn't a date? It took us an hour to tame your crazy long Rapunzel hair and make you presentable before you went home." I lowered my voice. "Do you think he has erectile dysfunction or something?"

She huffed and made her way to the other side of the rack of jackets we were flipping through. "If he does, I wouldn't know anything about it. He'd have to actually try to put his dick in me for that."

"So, nothing happened?"

"Yeah, that's what I said," she nearly snarled. "Absolutely nothing happened."

"Look, Snappy McSnapperson, forgive me, but it is Rayonus we're talking about. Something had to have happened. I think it's illegal for him not to do something untoward. It's against his demonic code of douchebaggery or something."

Ignoring me, she handed me a black leather jacket that wasn't my style at all. "Try this on. I want to borrow it tomorrow night."

I raised a brow. "A few additions to your wardrobe, huh?"

"Hey, the demon owes me. Who am I not to take advantage of that?"

"Will you hush?" I hissed, grabbing her arm and rushing her away from a bewildered Harlow Augustine who was flipping through a rack of shirts next to us. "I think she might've heard you! You know her grandmother is a Court member!"

"Oh, please!" Penelope said, waving away my panic. "Anyone that knows me probably thinks I'm talking about Ray. If anyone is really a demon in this town, I think we're all in agreement that it's him."

I tilted my head, thinking about the way Ray looked, acted, and skulked around town like he was casing the joint, and shrugged. "You know, I think you may have a point."

Loaded down with shopping bags full of skirts, tops, and whatever else we thought we could get away with, Penelope and I walked out of Callie's Consignments feeling slightly guilty over the amount of

Cam's money we'd spent but excited to replenish our stock of shared clothes.

I'd broken down mid–shopping trip and called Cam to confess our shopping sins; after feigning anger for half a second, he'd told me to have a good time, but not that good of a time. Since becoming a full incubus and gaining the power to steal an entire soul from a human instead of just a part, I'd asked him to scale back the number of clients he took, so money was tighter than it had been at the beginning of our relationship.

He didn't have to tell us twice. After all the stress of dealing with Cam's demon shit, my demon shit, and Ray's lovable yet aggravating demon shit, we needed to relax, and shopping was a good start. We'd see how sideways the day would go from there.

"So, I'm thinking wine and a girly movie night," I said, pointing Penelope to the snow-covered blue SUV Cam had insisted I buy for the times he was out of town.

She shrugged. "That sounds good. But you know what sounds better?"

"What?" I asked tentatively. With Penelope, you never knew what crazy plan she'd come up with. "Will prison stripes be involved?"

She continued as if I hadn't spoken. "Picture it, Mavis. Me and you, *Supernatural*—"

"Naturally," I interrupted.

She glared at me and hissed, "I'm working on a theme here!"

"Oh, pardon me," I said, unlocking the doors and popping the back hatch open with the key fob. "Do go on."

She met my eyes over the top of the car and squinted. "Next time, I'll just lead with the tequila, *Supernatural* hater."

"Hey!" I retorted, following her into the car to defend myself. "I am not a *Supernatural* hater. I just don't get all freaky about it like you do."

"Freaky?" she asked, laughing as she buckled her seatbelt.

"Frea-kay," I assured her. "You can love *Supernatural*, but you shouldn't LOVE *Supernatural*."

She put on her sunglasses and refused to look at me. "Everything you just said is wrong, and I hate you."

I chuckled and pulled away from the curb. "So, tequila, you say?"

Three hours later, we were back at the apartment, pleasantly buzzed and starting season fourteen of *Supernatural* with Rayonus. Like clockwork, he had shown up as soon as we came home. I was beginning to think he was tracking Penelope with GPS. He was rarely here when she wasn't.

"Who wants another shot?" I asked, clumsily getting to my feet and stumbling over to the side table.

Ray stood up and quickly wrested control of the bottle before I could spill it everywhere—again. "Penelope?" he asked. "Fancy one?"

"Shhh," she said, too engrossed in Castiel's ambush by demons to be bothered.

"That's a yes," I told him.

He grinned, his straight teeth glinting in the light of the television. "You guys need some food to soak up all this alcohol." He checked his watch. "And I've got the perfect thing. I'll be right back."

Penelope unexpectedly turned her attention away from the TV. "If you bring me tacos, Ray, I will reward you with unspeakable acts using only my tongue."

Rayonus let out a nervous little laugh and ran a hand through his dark hair. "Yeah, you guys need food."

When the door closed behind a weirdly skittish Ray, I whirled on Penelope. "Unspeakable things with your tongue? What the actual fuck?"

"I know!" she exclaimed, groaning in humiliation and flopping down onto the floor. "I don't know what is wrong with me."

"Alexa, pause," I said, stopping the show on the streaming device and joining Penny on the floor. "Penny—"

She grimaced. "You know I hate it when you call me that."

"No, you don't. You hate it when Rayonus calls you that. Just like he hates it when you call him Ray."

"What's your point?"

"My point is that you guys are one hundred percent hot for each other. Look at how he's acting around you tonight. This choir boy routine is disturbingly abnormal for him. I honestly think you guys need more alone time together so you can figure out the next step in this weird love affair thing you have going on." I snapped my fingers when inspiration suddenly hit. "We can go camping! The temperature is supposed to be a balmy thirty-two degrees over the weekend. That's nearly unheard of for March. And I know you're off from Sakura those days. It's perfect!"

She scrunched up her pretty face and sat up. "There is nothing perfect about camping."

"You can't tell me that you don't want to cozy up in a two-person sleeping bag with a certain sexy demon to keep warm."

Penelope chewed her lip. "Yeah, but I don't have a two-person sleeping bag."

I waved away her excuse. "Backwoods Sport & Ski will likely have one in stock. You're just coming up with excuses, and you know it."

"Are you sure this sudden need for outdoorsy fun doesn't have anything to do with the fact that the six months Severin gave you in exchange for Cam's soul are nearly up? And that he's going to come looking to collect you soon, and you don't have a clue how to get rid of the protection amulet that keeps you from shanking his sorry ass?" she asked.

"Yes . . . no." I frowned. "Okay, maybe, but it also has everything to do with you and Rayonus finally putting the nail in this coffin, so to speak."

"What about wild animals?"

I sat up and selected a lime slice for a chaser. "Besides the one that could potentially be in your panties this weekend?"

"You know what I mean, weirdo."

"And you know what I mean. What are you afraid of?"

She feigned thought. "Getting hurt by a demon with a deliciously huge cock?"

I choked and sputtered on the shot of tequila I'd just taken. "How do you know Rayonus has a huge cock?"

"I might have seen the outline of it in his sweats the other morning when he slept on my couch. Oh, and he's mentioned it a couple hundred times this week."

"Here," I said, handing her a refilled shot glass. "Drink a few more of these, and you won't care how big that demon cock is. You'll climb on that thing like it's Mount Everest."

"Who's climbing onto a Mount Everest demon cock?" Cam asked, shaking snow out of his short hair as he closed the front door behind him.

"Me. Now that you're home," I said, staggering into his arms and reveling in his clean, manly scent for a moment before I grinned up at him.

He shook his head as he took in Penelope laying on the floor and my drunken state. "I see you ladies started the party without me."

"If someone would've told me he was coming home, we would've waited," I said, lifting onto my toes to give him a kiss.

Cam groaned and ran his hands down to cup my ass, then hitched me up to let me wrap my legs around him. He deepened the kiss, thrusting his tongue into my mouth in a hypnotic, teasing way that made me do a little groaning myself. When he broke the kiss, he leaned his forehead to mine, breathing heavily. "I missed you, Mavis."

I stroked the side of his face. "I missed you, too, baby. Now, kick Penny out, so you can take me in the back and fuck me until I scream."

Cam grinned wickedly and pulled me tight against his erection, making me whimper. "Tell me what you want," he growled. "And I'll give it to you."

"Hey!" Penelope exclaimed. "You guys are just being rude! Some of us aren't getting any, you know!"

"What's rude is not letting your best friends have an orgasm in their own bed," Cam spat back. "So help me, Penelope, if you don't let me fuck my bride-to-be tonight, I'm putting a deposit down on a house in Havenwood Heights."

"Fine," she snapped. "Have your unnatural monkey sex, Cam, but don't say I didn't warn you when Ray wants to join you for a threesome."

We all turned around as a throat cleared and the front door closed. Ray grinned in delight at the spectacle in front of him and held up two bags from the Tacos for Daze truck. "Who's hungry?"

"Me!" I said, unlocking my legs and sliding down to the carpet, leaving Cam scrambling to cover his erection.

Ray smirked and handed over the bags, sitting on the couch next to where Penelope sat on the floor. Smiling down at her, he asked, "What's this about a threesome?"

CHAPTER 3

*A*fter a little pouting, a lot of begging, and a whole fuckload of shots, Penelope and I finally got Cam and Rayonus to agree to go camping over the weekend.

Well, to be precise, I got Rayonus to agree after I cornered him to mention the potential of happy naked fun time he could have while alone with Penelope, and once I told Cam I'd be chaperoning them whether he came with us or not, he knew he really didn't have a choice in the matter. Longtime friend or not, there was no way he'd send an untrustworthy demon like Ray out into the woods with the two of us, especially with his father's deadline coming up in the next few weeks.

To say Cam wasn't happy about the camping trip would be an understatement. He sighed every time we mentioned it. He only grunted when I asked him if he wanted me to pack for him. He downright refused to go to the store with us for provisions. He basically just sucked the fun out of the whole thing and made me a cranky mess.

"This camping trip was supposed to be fun," I griped for the hundredth time since we'd arrived at Backwoods Sport & Ski.

Penelope, not wanting to deal with me, made a beeline to the lanterns to avoid my whining, leaving Rayonus to talk me down from the tree this time.

"Whatever you're worried about, it's nothing, Mavis," he said, wrapping a companionable arm around my shoulders. "Cam's irritation has little to do with you. It's Severin who's causing his stress. How can he relax on a nice camping trip when the last time you trekked out into the woods together, you had to kill your grandfather, and he had to stand up to his father, which ultimately cost him his soul? Not to mention, his father or his underlings are sure to be lurking out there somewhere to keep an eye on you. Can you see why he might be more than a little uncomfortable with the idea?"

"Yes," I grumbled. "But can you please stop making sense?"

He ruffled my hair. "Come on, Mavis. Cheer up. You know he'd do anything for you and Penelope. Give him a little credit."

"I'll try," I muttered.

"You should." He smiled, but it didn't reach his eyes. "Not all of us demons have the capacity for good that he does."

I squinted at him, not quite understanding him, but I asked, "When did you get all insightful about this kind of stuff?"

"I didn't," he said, shrugging. "I just want you two to pull your shit together, so I can get some alone time with Penelope. After that panty comment the other day, I think she's starting to cave on her sex-with-demons embargo."

We set out for our hike up Mount Mae late on Saturday morning. Though Penelope and I made a show of pouting and glancing forlornly at the ski resort and its promise of hot chocolate and warmth as we drove past, an unmoved Cam reminded me that this was my idea, continued on, and parked at Danzan Park to start our trek up the long snowy trail he said would take us to several good places that he'd camped before. It was cold, and the wind was brisk, but it was nothing we weren't accustomed to, living in the high altitudes of Colorado. Not that that kept Penelope from complaining about it—and then complaining about how many times Rayonus offered to "warm her up." Cam and I didn't speak much on the climb up the mountain, opting to stay out of reach of Penelope's bad mood, but we were making our own conversation with rolled eyes, commiserating glances, and shrugs as we listened to our two besties bicker like an old married couple.

We'd only been hiking through the calf-deep snow for an hour or so when Rayonus spotted what I thought was the perfect camping spot. The meadow he found was surrounded by trees and brush that had obviously been cleared since the last snowfall, and there was even a stone fire pit ready for us to use for our requisite marshmallow and hot dog roast. It was perfect.

"I don't think we're going to find a better place than this," I told the group, letting my backpack slide to the ground beside me. "Nice going, Rayonus."

He bowed. "My pleasure, Mavis."

Penelope rolled her eyes, still irritated. "Next time, find a spot with spa services."

"If you're interested in a facial, I think I can . . ."

Cam stepped between them before the situation could get any uglier than it already was, turning his back on Ray. "Penelope, can you help Mavis find some firewood while Rayonus and I set up the tents?

"I think foraging in the woods should be the guy's job," she said through clenched teeth. "Mavis and I can set up the tents."

I shot a significant look at Cam. Clearly, Penelope was on edge. When she got like this, it was best to let her have her way until she was done venting.

He held up his hands in defeat, slapped Rayonus on the

shoulder, and they made their way toward the path just up the hill without another word.

"Why do I like him?" Penelope asked. "He's disgusting."

"No, he's not," I told her, handing her the tent parts as I took them out of the bag. "He's inappropriate in public, but I've never heard him say anything that Cam doesn't say to me in private. Honestly, I think Cam is way nastier than Ray is. He has a lot more practice."

"Ew."

"Oh, you love that dirty talk. Don't act like you don't. You'll be thinking about Ray coming on your face for the rest of the day."

She looked stricken. "Fuck me," she groaned.

I chuckled. "I think Ray has that particular activity covered."

"Oh, ha ha," she said, shaking her head.

"Listen, Penny, I'm going to be brutally honest with you. I'm worried that you really are going to end up that crusty old waitress with the twelve cats that everyone talks about in town. I'm also worried that Rayonus is going to become boring without his charm and blatant sexual come-ons if you keep snapping his head off. So, lighten the fuck up, okay? Flirt a little, for goodness' sake. Don't forget we need Ray around for comedic relief. We sure as hell won't be getting it from Cameron this weekend."

"You're right. I'll lighten up."

"And?"

She sighed. "And I'll try to flirt without hyperventilating or punching him in the dick."

"That's all I ask," I said, laughing as I looked at what we'd unpacked. "Do you know what the fuck any of this is?"

She picked up a short metal rod and shrugged. "I have no idea. I just didn't want to go into the woods. There are wild animals in there, remember?"

I wriggled my eyebrows. "You mean besides Ray?"

She smacked me on the shoulder. "Shut up and tell me how we're supposed to put up these tents."

I stood and brushed the fresh snow off my knees. "I don't have the first clue, but I do have an idea I've been working on that might work even better than these flimsy tents."

"What kind of an idea?" she asked warily. "I've seen this look on your face before. This could either go really right or really, really wrong."

"I'm thinking about making an igloo."

She stared at me in amazement. "Like, from the Arctic Circle place in Finland?"

"Like that, yeah. But without the amenities. You'll have to get your facial the old-fashioned way," I said, laughing and jumping back when she tried to smack me again.

"And you'll be doing this with your magic, I suppose?" she asked.

I shrugged. "Why not? Ever since the throttle holding back my magic broke open, I'm practically Queen Elsa over here."

"You're going be a hit at all of the parties in the summer," she joked. "We'll never have to send someone on an emergency trip for ice."

"Funny," I told her, my tone frosty.

She grinned. "Well, it's true!"

"And still not funny," I said, squinting at her.

"Fine, fine. Let's build an igloo. How can I help?"

I pointed toward the path Cam and Ray had taken. "Go stand over there."

"That's it?"

"Pretty much. There's not much to it. The basic principle is easy. I just need to use my magic to dig out a circle in the snow, make ice blocks that angle slightly at the top, stack the ice blocks, leaving a way for the smoke to get out, and strengthen it with ice and snow. I think I've got this. I've tried things like this before, just on a way, way smaller scale."

"Well, give it a go," she said, glancing warily at the woods behind her. "It sounds a hell of a lot safer than a tent out here in the open."

"It is," I told her, walking around until I found the flattest spot. "It's warmer, too, because it'll retain our body heat."

"You had me at 'warmer,'" she said, her teeth chattering as the wind kicked up. "Fuck, it's cold up here now that we've stopped hiking."

"Give me a sec," I said, closing my eyes and raising my arms to push my magic forward.

Freeing myself of the control I'd worked so hard to master over the past five months, I started out slow, going through the steps with more concentration than I'd ever given anything in my life. I was careful that every detail was taken into consideration before I finally opened my eyes to see what Penelope had been softly gasping at since I'd started.

And when I opened my eyes—holy shit. It had worked. Before us stood a gigantic igloo, wrapped heavily in snow and looking as sturdy as the mountain itself.

"You did it!" Penelope crowed, dancing around the igloo like she didn't have a care in the world before falling backward to make snow angels. "That was the most amazing thing I've ever seen!"

"I leave you for ten minutes, and I come back to a delirious human and a giant-sized igloo," Cam admonished, walking out of the woods with Ray, a huge load of branches in each of their arms. "What am I going to do with you, little ice demon?"

I grinned and skipped over to him. "If you're thinking punishment, you could save one of these switches for later."

"You can bet your sweet sore ass that I will," he growled, swatting me with his free hand.

"Maybe I should set up our tent inside the igloo," Ray said to

Penelope, offering her a hand up from the snow. "We may need it, so we don't see something that scars us for life."

"Maybe we'll be the ones to scar them for life," Penelope retorted. "I did promise to perform unspeakable things on you the other night.".

Ray swallowed hard and seemed unable to speak for a few seconds while all the blood from his brain rushed to his dick. "Trust me, Penny. I haven't forgotten."

"No one is going to scar anyone," I told them, laughing at Ray's shell-shocked appearance. "The igloo is divided into thirds. We're on the left. You guys are on the right. We can put the fire pit in the middle, toward the front. We won't even have to see each other after we go to bed."

"Why did 'go to bed' seem like it was in special sexy quotations?" Cam asked quietly.

"I'm seriously disappointed that you have to ask," I teased, nipping him on the lips before sashaying toward the igloo.

CHAPTER 4

By three o'clock in the afternoon, we had unpacked what we could and were settled around the fire to cook a well-deserved late lunch of hot dogs and coffee from our thermoses. Everyone was in high spirits, especially Penelope. I think the prospect of staying in a tent on a mountainside was stressing her out more than being in one with an actual demon who was trying to get in her pants. With the relative safety of the igloo, she seemed much happier, which meant there was a good chance of Ray feeling much happier later on when they were alone.

We had been chatting good-naturedly about the weather, the ridiculous depth of the snow on the mountain, and how superior igloos were to tents for only a few minutes when Penelope suddenly blurted out, "Guys! We should play Three Questions!"

I raised my brows. "Three Questions?" I asked. "With this group?"

"Well, why not? I played it all the time when I was a kid. It's a good icebreaker."

When no one in the group showed the proper enthusiasm for her suggestion, she huffed and snapped, "It'll distract me from the

23

lack of TV in front of me, okay? So make with the questions, demons."

"What is Three Questions?" asked a confused Ray.

"It's a children's getting-to-know-you game," Cam answered.

"When it's your turn, each of the other players gets to ask you a question," I added. "It's pretty simple and definitely better with booze involved."

"What do I win?"

Penelope's eyes twinkled with humor. "You win knowledge about the human and demons you've been living and hanging around with for the past few months, oh man of mystery."

Ray made a sour face. "This does sound like it'd be better with booze."

"Well, it just so happens, I brought booze," Cam said, getting up to rummage through his backpack. "Fireball or vodka, take your pick."

I clapped my hands together in excitement and joined him where he'd temporarily stowed our things. "Have I told you that I love you lately, Cameron?"

"Yes, but I think that's something better shown than told," he said, leaning down to plant a soft kiss on my lips that spoke volumes about what was to come.

Penelope shuddered. "You guys are so gross!"

"Yeah," Ray agreed. "At least wait until we get a few shots in us before you start the sexy talk."

"This ancient wisdom is coming from you, the innuendo king?" I shot back, hands on hips. "Do my ears deceive me?"

Rayonus rolled his eyes and grabbed the bottle from a preoccupied Cam. "Penelope, hand me your mug. If we drink this really fast, we may not remember all the sordid details."

She shook her head. "I've tried, Ray. It never works."

"It's Rayonus," he reminded her.

"It's whatever I want it to be," she insisted. "Ray."

He smirked as he poured a healthy shot of Fireball, clearly up to something. "Fine, but just remember, I've seen your mail. I know your middle name. I can and will start using it if you keep this up. Penny."

"Fine," she conceded, accepting her filled mug from him. "But you just wait until it's my turn to ask you questions, buddy. I'm going to make you sweat."

"As hot as that sounds, you'd have to separate the two lovebirds first," he told her, grimacing at us as our cuddling took on a more sexual tone than we'd initially intended it to.

"You know we can hear and see you, right?" I asked, breaking away from Cam and his deliciously wicked mouth. "We're literally standing right across the igloo from you."

"Then you know you're holding up the game," Penelope griped. "Get back over here so we can get started."

Cam walked me back to the fire pit and handed me down into my little folding camp chair before sitting in his own next to me.

"Do you have any questions for me, Mavis?" he asked, his voice barely above a whisper.

The way he said my name sent a shiver of excitement through my body, and he smiled at the sight, his wolfish grin telling me that he'd seen my reaction and couldn't wait to make me do that again, preferably when we were both naked.

Penelope demanded that Rayonus answer two questions as soon as he chose the short stick. He grimaced at her, but we all knew he'd cave to her wishes. He was as close as he'd ever been to getting something he'd wanted since the day they met. Right now, he was putty in her hands.

As predicted, he gave up right away. "Fine, love," he said. "What do you want to know?"

She tapped her chin. "What's your favorite color and food?"

Rayonus's brows raised at the basic questions. "Is that all you want to know?"

Before she could answer, I said, "Don't get comfortable. I want to know what kind of demony stuff you do when you're not in Havenwood Falls."

Ray laughed and waved my interest in his secret personal life away with a careless hand. "You don't want me to bore you with tales from my mundane life. It's not as exciting as you'd think."

I wasn't about to give up on learning more about him so quickly. His open-ended stay at our apartment had been shrouded in mystery since he arrived. "Come on, Rayonus," I urged. "You've been living with us for months now. I know less than nothing about you. Tell us a little about yourself."

"Really, there's not much to tell," he hedged, looking to Cam for help with the tiniest amount of desperation in his expression.

Cam ignored his silent plea, apparently not interested in saving his friend from our interrogation. Instead, he handed me a stick with a hot dog pushed onto the end.

I promptly took the hot dog off and brandished the sharpened stick like a weapon. "Tell us your life story, Rayonus Rixa, or I'll poke you with a hot dog stick."

"Have you had her checked for rabies?" Ray asked Cam, while he leaned as far away from me as possible.

"I think you'd better answer her," Cam said, pushing a hot dog onto another stick without glancing up. "She can get a little stabby when she hasn't eaten."

"Stop being a little bitch, Rayonus," Penelope said, exasperated. "We're not asking for government secrets here."

Ray sighed. "Fine, but only because you used my name. He smirked and added, "And asked me so nicely."

She regally inclined her head.

"My favorite color is the beautiful brown shade of Penelope's eyes, my favorite food is potatoes, and . . ."

"What kind of potatoes?" Penelope interrupted. "You can't just say potatoes."

"Most women would have been flattered by my compliment. You're asking me whether I like mashed or fried?"

"Heck yeah," she said. "This may be deal breaker stuff."

"Deal breaker stuff?" he asked her. "I think I need some clarification."

Cam and I watched their conversational volleying, trying to contain our laughter. Seeing Penelope, a human, fluster a demon who was used to women fawning all over him was better than TV.

"Just answer her," Cam said finally. "Mashed or fried?"

"Fried with onions, actually."

Penelope scrunched up her face in disgust. "Ew. Why?"

He shrugged. "It's what I've eaten the most of. I've lived through some very lean times."

"What about the demon shit while you're out of town?" I asked, not wanting Penelope to delve deeper into the subject. It wasn't my finest conversational segue, but damn it, I wanted an answer.

Rayonus fidgeted with the mug in his hands, hesitating a moment before he answered, "I have . . . uh, business dealings that I tend to from time to time outside of town."

"What kind of 'business dealings'?" Penelope asked, making quotation marks with her fingers.

"The kind a nice human woman like you doesn't need to worry about," he answered.

She harrumphed. "So, it's something shady. What. A. Shocker."

He glowered at Penelope. "When is it your turn in the hot seat, young miss?"

"Right after Cameron asks you his question," I said, passing Ray a hot dog to roast. "Go ahead, Cam."

Cam studied his best demon friend for a moment, then he

asked a question none of us expected. "Are you here to hurt any of us, Rayonus?"

Startled, Penelope and I stared at Ray, waiting impatiently for his answer. I think in the back of our minds, we always wondered if Ray was in Havenwood Falls for some flagitious reason, but we were always too afraid to ask. Some questions you just didn't want an answer to.

"I have no desire to hurt anyone in Havenwood Falls, least of all you three," he answered, nonplussed. "No matter what you think of me now, or in the future, that has never been, and will never be, my intention."

"Good," Penelope said. "Because I didn't want to have to kick your ass, Ray."

Rayonus smirked at his tipsy love interest. "That is a relief, love."

"Okay!" I exclaimed, rubbing my hands with excited glee. "Now that that awkwardness is behind us, Penelope, you're up."

She sighed. "Just get it over with."

Cam snickered. "Is someone regretting suggesting this game?"

She held up her fingers to indicate *just a little* and asked, "Who's first?"

"I am," Ray said, rubbing his hands with glee. "Tell us, Penelope. Why aren't you dating anyone?"

She blushed and shifted her gaze from him to the fire. "I sort of am dating someone," she admitted.

Surprised at her honest answer, we all stared at her, waiting for her to continue.

"What?" she asked. "Can't I like a guy?"

"Who is he?" Rayonus inquired. His voice was soft and barely above a whisper. He was obviously hurt by her confession.

I sighed. "You, dumbass. You haven't noticed that you two are in a relationship?"

"Shouldn't both parties know that they are in the

relationship?" he asked Penelope, who looked like she'd rather be out in the cold than getting pleasantly buzzed around a fire with her best friends.

She threw her hands up. "You keep asking me out. You spend ninety percent of your downtime with me. Not to mention, you treat trying to get into my pants like it's an Olympic sport and you're going for the gold medal. You don't call that dating?"

Rayonus didn't say anything as he pondered over his past actions. He knew she was right. It was clear as day that they both liked each other and wanted more.

"You're right," he said finally. "I do like you. I just wasn't sure if you were okay with a casual fling. You're not the type of girl that sleeps around with no strings attached."

"Is that all you want?" she asked.

"No," he said truthfully. "But right now, that's all I can give you." When he saw the hurt look on her face, he quickly added, "It's not as if I don't want more. You're a very welcome surprise that I didn't expect to find when I came to visit my old friend."

Slightly mollified, she nodded and turned her attention back to the fire. "Fair enough."

"Well, that was fucking painfully awkward," I said. "Next question, Cam?"

Cameron tapped his chin for a moment, then asked, "What's it like to have demons for friends instead of regular humans?"

"There's nothing 'regular' about most of the people in this town," Penelope replied.

"What do you mean?" Ray asked.

"I mean, there are a shit ton of not-so-human folks running around Havenwood Falls. Haven't you noticed?"

"Why would I? I don't have the soul-detecting magic Cameron does." He stopped talking and stared at her. "Wait. How do you know?"

"Then what is your demon power?" I asked, distracting him so that Penelope could keep her little secret if she so desired. "You've never said anything about it."

Ray took a deep breath and pursed his lips, looking away from us.

"Is it that bad?" Penelope asked.

"I guess that depends on your perspective. My magic isn't as cut and dried as Cameron's. I cause discord, havoc, destruction. One touch of my hand on a person, or really, any being, and I could destroy every hope, every dream you've ever had." He held up his hands and stared at them. "I may not be able to kill demons with these, as Mavis can, but for every other object, my hands were made to destroy them, either emotionally or physically."

My mouth fell open. "How do you keep it under control? Cam has women falling all over themselves when he's out in public."

"My Court-issued tattoo keeps the people in Havenwood Falls safe, but outside of the town, I have to keep a constant vigil over my magic. If I let any part of it slip out, there's no telling what will be unleashed."

With a note of fear in her voice, Penelope asked, "So, you don't sleep? You're constantly keeping it suppressed."

Rayonus pulled a delicate ebony charm attached to a brown leather string out of his collar. "When I'm around you, this allows me to sleep. I don't dare trust the coven's magic alone. You are too important to me."

I rolled my eyes. "And you thought you weren't in a relationship. Pu-lease."

Cam laughed. "Oh, he's definitely smitten. He hasn't told a female about his affliction in the eighty years I've known him."

"It's been much longer than eighty years since I've shared this part of myself with a woman," Ray told his friend. "Much, much longer."

Penelope's eyes bugged at that little piece of information. "*How* long have you guys known each other?"

"Since Cameron was a young man. I worked for his father before he went over to the dark side."

"So, that makes you how old?" she pressed.

He reached out and stroked Penelope's cheek. "Promise you won't run screaming from the room?"

She barked out a sharp laugh. "No way."

"Just tell her," Cam said. "You've put it off too long as it is."

Rayonus sighed and reached for the bottle of cinnamon-flavored whiskey I offered. "I turned six hundred and three years old last Thursday." He took a swig from the uncapped bottle and handed it to Penny. "Freaked out yet?"

She accepted the bottle, then stood, motioning for me to join her. "Mavis? A word, please?"

I scrambled out of my chair and followed her outside the igloo, confused. She'd known that Cameron was over a century old and that Rayonus was likely just as old, if not older. Could his revelation be that shocking to her, or was it something else?

"What's going on?" I asked, giving her my jacket when her teeth immediately started chattering. With my ice magic, it felt like it was seventy-two degrees on the mountain.

"I can't fuck a demon that's nearly a thousand years old, Mavis."

Intrigued, I asked, "And why is that?"

"What do you mean, 'why is that'? What if he thinks I'm some inexperienced virgin?"

I laughed and took the whiskey from her hand, taking a swig of it. "What? Has your hymen grown back? Did you forget what goes where? How long has it been, Penny?"

She glared at me. "You know what I mean, asshole. I'm an infant compared to him. He's probably invented sex positions."

"Or he's just as nervous about it as you are. Don't you remember his reaction to your tongue comment earlier? He looked like he was going to sink through the ground. Where was Mr. Confident Lovemaker then?"

She wrinkled her nose and took the whiskey back. "Can you never use that name again? It skeeves me out. It sounds like something my foster mom would say."

"Well, stop acting like a mousy introvert, and I won't have to use mom words. This isn't you. Where's the loudmouth, sarcastic bitch we all know and tolerate?"

"Point taken," she said, sighing heavily. "Do you think he's going to think I'm ridiculous now?"

"No, I think he's going to take you up on your tongue offer if you'll get in there and stop worrying about nothing. You've got this."

"What about you?" she asked. "Are you and Cam cool? He seems a lot less keyed up."

I bit my lip and twisted my engagement ring on my finger. "I hope so. He hasn't seemed antsy or weird since we arrived, but I know he's still worried."

Penelope wrapped me in a hug. "We'll get the old Cam back, Mavis. And we'll kick Severin's ass back to whatever part of hell he's from for good. Stop worrying."

"I wish I could, Penny. I really wish I could."

CHAPTER 5

*W*e stayed up late, sitting around the fire and talking about nothing until the many desirous looks a quiet Cam was shooting in my direction from the other side of the fire became impossible to ignore. Making our excuses, we bid our friends good night and were out of sight in a flash. Cam hadn't been able to slake his lust since the night before, and I knew that, by now, he'd be hardcore jonesing for sex, especially since alcohol only fueled his hunger.

As expected, Cam pounced on me as soon as we were alone, his eyes soulless and black as he pressed me to the icy wall and kissed me hard. I shivered, though I couldn't feel the cold. When Cam was channeling his incubus lust like this, he unnerved me as much as he tempted me. I wanted him, but I couldn't help but be a little intimidated.

In my heart, I knew Cam was a good, decent man, but the past five months without a soul had made him almost cold at times. I knew tonight would be no different. The pure animal need on his beautifully cruel face told me I would be in for one hell of a ride . . . or ten.

Gripping my hips, he dragged me closer, his erection unforgiving as it dug into my stomach. "Do you want my cock, ice demon?"

"Shhh," I whispered. "They'll hear us."

"Let them hear," he said, ripping my jeans open with the superhuman strength he rarely displayed. I gasped as he yanked them down my thighs and spun me to face away from him.

Snaking a hand between my legs, he bit down on the tender spot where my neck and shoulder joined hard enough to make me yelp. "I asked you a question."

"Yes," I moaned, now fully into whatever hurried, dirty sex he wanted.

His voice was harsh as he hissed, "Take your demon shape."

I complied, willingly morphing to the form I knew he preferred, and arched my back, wanting him to claim me, to ravage me until I couldn't think about all the problems waiting for us at home.

"Cam, please," I begged.

"On your knees," he demanded.

I obeyed, dropping down to the sleeping bag we'd set out earlier, nearly shaking with the anticipation of feeling the fullness of his massive cock inside of me.

The slow slide of his zipper and the thump of his belt buckle hitting the floor sounded loud in my ears as I waited. I'd thought he'd take me quickly, but he seemed to be weighing his options as if he was having a hard time choosing what would bring him the most pleasure.

That was when I felt the first stinging strike of the switch across both cheeks. The pain was sharp but exquisite, making my breath catch and my center dampen with want. "Please," I cried out, needing more.

A breath I didn't know I'd been holding escaped in a quick whoosh as he brought the switch down twice in quick succession. I squirmed involuntarily to move away from the pain, and Cam chuckled as he sank to his knees beside me, running a soft hand over the burning welts before slapping my ass so hard, it brought tears to my eyes.

"Have you had enough?" he asked, his voice little more than a growl.

"Never," I told him defiantly.

"Be careful what you ask for, beauty," he warned, pressing his hard cock against my hip as he trailed the scratchy wood across the same path his fingers had taken. "I like hearing you scream."

"Then make me scream," I said, bracing myself.

He brushed over my clit with the thumb of his free hand, teasing me with the pleasure that was to come. "I can make you scream in other ways," he said, whipping the switch across my ass again.

"Fuck me!" I cried out. "Please."

Cam chuckled darkly and thrummed his thumb against my clit again. "You are so beautiful when you beg, Mavis. I almost want to give you what you want."

I glanced behind me and gave him a sultry smile. "Then why don't you, big boy?"

He sucked in a deep breath through his teeth as he looked at my reddened ass. "Do you think you can handle this while I'm in my demon form?" he asked, stroking his cock. "It's a little bigger than you're used to."

I froze. He'd only ever shown me what he looked like as an incubus once. Though I knew he could transform his appearance to any humanoid thing, since he'd gained the ability, he'd always maintained the form he was born in while he was with me.

"Mavis?"

"Show me," I said, turning over to sit, then hissing in pain.

"How's that ass feeling?" Cam asked, a devilish grin spreading across his handsome face.

I kicked off my boots and shimmied out of my jeans. "You tell me."

"Pretty fucking good, darling."

"Damn right it does," I said sassily. "Now make with the demon form and give me my well-deserved orgasm before I go get it elsewhere."

He narrowed his eyes. "You wouldn't."

"Wouldn't I?"

He shook his head. "You are a bad, bad girl. You deserved every lick of that switch and then some."

I leaned up to kiss him. "I loved every lick of that switch. I'm thinking of taking it home with us."

"You do that, and I'm using it every chance I get," he promised, pushing me to my back and settling between my legs.

I smirked. "Can't wait."

He rocked against my wetness, groaning with restraint. "Are you sure about this?"

"More than sure," I said. "I'm a demon. You're a demon. We should be having lots of demon sex by now."

"What do you call all the sex we had before?"

"Foreplay?"

He laughed, showing sharp fangs. "So, this is our first time?"

"You could say that," I said, watching as his skin and hair changed to a darker hue and his cheekbones became more pronounced. Even with the black eyes, he was so beautiful as a demon, I could scarcely believe he was real.

"Well?" he asked lifting himself to show me the complete transformation.

My eyes widened as I took in his body. He was taller, much more muscular, and his cock was . . . well, huge. "Fuck, Cameron. I don't know whether to run screaming or to tell you to do your worst with that thing."

"I can make it smaller."

"Don't you fucking dare. I'm going to ride you like a horse."

He laughed. "I'm glad you approve."

"Oh, this is more than approval. This is your ten-second warning to get that dick in me before I take matters into my own hands."

Eyes flared, he dove for me, driving into me in one quick, crazed movement that had me crying out into his mouth as I became accustomed to the increased size.

"So. Fucking. Tight," he whispered, withdrawing then snapping his hips to sink back into me. "I could come right now."

I moaned and dug my fingers into his ass as the first twinges of my own orgasm shot through my body. "Come with me, Cam."

I didn't have to ask him twice. Roaring, he hitched my legs up and pounded into me faster and harder than he ever had before. I closed my eyes tight, reveling in the new feel of him, the sound of his breath, harsh and shallow in my ears, and the sweet taste of cinnamon on his tongue as he kissed me carefully through his fangs. Soon, my quiet whimpers of pleasured pain became all-out screams as I writhed and shuddered under him, and we barreled over the edge.

When our breathing had calmed, Cam lifted his head from the crook of my neck and looked at me with an expression I'd never seen before.

"What is it?" I asked, stroking his hair back and then groaning as he flexed his hips to drive his semi-hard length deeper into me.

"I love you," he said, through clenched teeth.

I laughed. "I sure hope so. I mean, you have your penis in me, and more important than that, you've asked me to marry you."

Cam smiled, but it didn't reach his eyes. "No, I mean . . . I don't know what I mean. I guess I just thought it was the man in me that loved you, that couldn't live without you, but it's not. Even without a soul, I love you, Mavis. You're everything to me."

I looked deep into the black eyes that, until now, had been

devoid of any emotion. "And I love you, Cameron DeSalle. But this really shouldn't be a surprise. I've loved you all these months, and I've never had a soul. Love is love. It's a feeling, not something tied to humanity."

He pursed his lips. "You seem pretty sure of that."

"Of course I do." I glanced down to where we were joined and smirked. "But honestly, I'd probably say anything to keep this big demon dick in me right now. Holy shit, babe. You've been holding out on me for the last five months."

Cam grinned and buried himself as deep as he could go. "Trust me. I won't be holding out on you from here on out. You'll be lucky if I let you out of bed."

"You have to let her out of bed," Penelope called. "It's illegal to keep a sex slave in the state of Colorado."

"Yeah," Rayonus agreed. "I'm not bailing your ass out of jail. I don't think Sheriff Kasun likes me very much."

Stricken, Cam and I stared at each other in horror.

"Do you think they heard everything?" I asked, mortified.

"Every single bit of it," Ray said. "Nice work with that switch. It sounded like she really enjoyed it."

Penelope made a gagging sound. "I'm pretty sure I'm going to need therapy for PTSD after this."

CHAPTER 6

*J*erked awake sometime before daybreak and sat up. Something was wrong—really wrong. An odd feeling of foreboding wound through my entire body.

"Mavis!" Penelope hissed, running into our part of the igloo. "Wake up! Something is out there!"

Cam jumped up and turned on the camp light, only to realize he was still in his demon form and still as naked as the day he was born.

"What the fuck?" Penelope yelled, covering her eyes, then smacking into the icy wall when she couldn't see. "You're both naked. And demoned out! And are those wings, Cam?"

"Sorry, Penny!" Cam said, jamming his legs into his jeans as he morphed back into his human shape.

Ray snickered as he came around the wall to see what was going on. "Nice tits, Mavis."

"Get out, Ray!" I yelled, pulling the sleeping bag up to cover myself while frantically looking for the shirt Cam had quietly torn off my body after our sarcastic friends stopped giggling about our sex life and went to bed.

"What's going on?" Cam asked Penelope.

"I went outside to pee and heard loud rustling and something tromping through the snow. It's something huge, by the sound of it. What if it's a bear?"

"Do you think it's a shifter or a regular animal?"

"How the fuck would I know?" Penelope asked.

"You always know," Cam deadpanned. "It's literally your gift."

"Yeah, but I'm not going out there and getting close enough to check! I'm not an idiot!"

Now fully dressed, I wrapped an arm around a thoroughly worked up Penelope and led her back to the fire to sit with Ray. "Everyone needs to calm down. I'll seal off the igloo, okay? Whatever it is, it won't be able to get in here."

"But I still have to pee," she whined.

"Okay, why don't you take Ray with you?"

"Me?" Ray asked. "Why not Cameron?"

"What is he going to do if that thing attacks? Fuck it to death? Take off your little talisman and go destroy whatever's out there."

"That's pretty risky, Mavis," Rayonus admitted. "I could destroy something else without meaning to. And what if it's a demon? Wouldn't she be safer with you?"

"And put her at risk of Severin grabbing them both?" Cam asked incredulously. "No fucking way."

"Well, someone has to go with her," I told them. "She's not going out there alone."

Penelope stood up, a determined glint in her chocolate-brown eyes. "We'll all go."

Cam sat down in his camping chair. "I'm not going out there to watch you pee."

"Yes, the hell, you are," she retorted. "Get up. Now."

Grumbling under his breath, Cam stood and zipped up his jacket. "Why are we friends again?"

She scoffed. "My awesome personality. Obviously."

Ray grinned as he wrapped a scarf around his neck. "This may be the weirdest thing I've done in three centuries."

I shrugged, thinking this was just par for the course in our strange little friendship with Penelope. "Seems like a regular Sunday to me."

~

Around ten o'clock, we packed up the igloo to leave. After the anticlimactic outcome of the bear situation the night before, we were all tired and ready to go home. The only problem was, I didn't know what to do with the igloo now that we were done with it. I could produce and manipulate ice, but I couldn't change it once it was made or make it melt.

"Maybe we could just leave it," Penelope suggested.

I shook my head. "What if someone's in there when it starts to melt? It could collapse on top of them."

"I can do it," Ray offered. "But I'll need you guys to be at least fifty yards away when I do it. The talisman is going to have to come off."

Brows raised, I asked, "What's going to happen?"

"In a perfect scenario, it will crumble where it stands."

"And in a not perfect scenario?" Cam asked.

"The mountain crumbles."

Penelope slipped her backpack onto her shoulders and started down the trail. "And that's my cue to get the hell out of Dodge. See you guys."

Cam watched her hightail it down the mountain with a surprised expression on his handsome face. "She's really going to go by herself?"

I blew out an undignified raspberry. "No. The second she remembers that there are wild animals out here, she'll be back."

"I don't know," he said. "She's already gotten pretty far."

"I'll bet you twenty bucks."

"You're on," Cam said, spitting into his hand to shake.

I stared at his hand in disgust. "Yeah, that's not happening."

"I'll take that bet," Ray said, spitting in his hand.

The two demons shook on it, and Cam said, "You're on."

Ray smirked. "I think you're going to regret this one, Cameron."

"You sound sure of yourself, but you forget, I've known Penelope Osbourne for many, many years."

"I don't have to know her for years," Ray told him. "I spent last night with her after she thought she heard a bear in the woods. I know she's not going down this mountain by herself."

As if it were planned, almost as soon as he finished speaking, Penelope came back into sight. "Are you guys coming?" she asked, her voice testy and impatient.

Giddy because of the win, Ray smiled at his would-be paramour and said, "Penny, I'd love to come with you . . . or on you. Really, I'll come anywhere you want me to. All you have to do is ask."

I laughed and patted Ray on the shoulder as I walked past him to meet a thoroughly irritated Penelope. "All right! The old Rayonus is back! I was hoping to hear some tasteless come-ons today."

Ray laughed and bowed. "Happy to oblige, ice demon."

"Hurry up," Cam grumbled, slapping a twenty-dollar bill into Ray's hand. "I'm fucking starving from all the sex I had last night that you didn't."

"Dick!" Ray called after him, pocketing the money.

"Yeah, that'd be what I gave Mavis nearly all night," Cam retorted without turning around. "I know it's been a while since you've used yours, but I didn't think you'd forgotten what it was used for altogether."

Ray huffed at his retreating form and yelled, "Fuck you, sex demon!"

"No, thanks," Cam said, throwing an arm around Penelope and me. "Mavis took care of that last night—and again this morning."

Ray was still shaking his head in exasperation when we stopped at the bottom of a small hill to wait on him but only hesitated a moment before he reached into his shirt to take off the talisman. As soon as it was over his head, he touched a finger to the igloo, and it fell like sand being dumped onto a beach. It just fell where it stood. I couldn't even tell where it had been seconds before.

"Wow," Penelope whispered, watching Rayonus put the talisman back over his neck.

I nodded in disbelief. "You took the word right out of my mouth."

Cam rolled his eyes, obviously jealous of Ray's superior power. "If you two ladies are done gawking, I can hear pizza calling my name."

Ray joined us, smiling at his handiwork. "They can't help but stare, Cameron. I'm fucking amazing."

"Yeah," Cam agreed. "An amazing asshole."

"Jealous?" he asked his friend.

Cam gritted his teeth before admitting, "Maybe just a little."

After another hour of insulting banter and ridiculous wagers, we dropped our gear off at the apartment and walked down Eighth Street to Napoli's. I could have wept when the glorious scent of cheese and garlicky goodness hit my nostrils. Spotting a big booth near the back of the surprisingly empty restaurant, we sat down, eager for Cokes and pizza all around.

"Dude, I would perform sexual favors for some of whatever that smell is," Penelope said, shooting a longing look toward the kitchen.

"I don't think that's a valid form of payment," Ray teased. "But if you want to perform sexual favors for me, I'd be happy to spring for your lunch."

Penelope laughed. "Don't tempt me, demon."

"Penelope, you have to stop offering sex for food," Cam admonished, frowning at her. "It's starting to be a thing with you."

"Until I get either food or sex, I'll do whatever the hell I want," she shot back, much to Ray's delight.

I smiled at my group's typically quarrelsome behavior, but as entertaining as they were, I couldn't shake the niggling feeling of menace that had plagued me since we sat down. The feel of it was so strong, it was almost making me nauseous. Breathing in deep through my nose, I exhaled through my mouth and said, "Guys, I feel like something is wrong."

Ray nodded in agreement. "Yeah, the waitress is taking forever."

I shook my head. "That's not what I mean. I feel something . . . something inherently evil."

"Cue the danger music," Penelope said, rolling her eyes.

"I'm being serious, Penny," I said, rubbing at the weird vibration in the center of my chest. "I felt this way last night when you woke me up for a few minutes, but it seems way stronger now."

"Could you still be worked up about the nonexistent bear?" Ray suggested.

I pursed my lips. "I'm not so sure it was a bear."

Cam furrowed his brow, looking concerned as he threaded his fingers with mine. "Why didn't you say anything last night, Mavis?"

"It was only a weird vibe then. I thought it was a fluke. But now, I think it may be something more—a warning, maybe. You don't think Severin could be back in town, do you?"

"Wouldn't someone warn you if dear old dad was back?" Penelope asked. "Isn't there some kind of tracking system that monitors who goes in and out of Havenwood Falls?"

Cam shrugged. "My father, yes. The coven would contact me at once. But any of his lackeys, probably not. I can imagine they would question them as soon as they sensed their arrival, but I doubt they could tell if a visitor was planning some kind of demon kidnapping unless they tell them they're going to do it. And I really don't think that's likely to happen, do you?"

"No," I muttered. "But wouldn't it be nice if one thing went our way for a change?"

CHAPTER 7

*E*arly the next morning, Cam and I visited Sheriff Kasun to
see if he knew something we didn't. It was, of course, a
bust. We knew it would be before we even arrived. Ric was good at
his job. He would have immediately contacted us if there was
something we needed to worry about, but to appease us, he did
promise to be on high alert on our behalf. After the mess with the
Collector this winter, no one in the town was taking any chances.

We went home after a quick breakfast at Eggstravaganza to talk
about what we were going to do on the days he had to go out of
town. We both knew Severin would make his move soon. There was
no way he'd wait out the entire six months he'd promised. That was
out of the question. He knew he'd have a fight on his hands.

After talking most of the day about contingency plans, safety,
and options, we realized, as much as we wanted it, the one option
we couldn't afford was Cameron staying at home with me for an
extended time. He had to see his clients to pay the rent. That was
non-negotiable, no matter how much he didn't want to leave me
alone.

What was negotiable was how far I was willing to go to help

Cam take his mind off the impending doom while simultaneously making the most of his incubus abilities. Since our romp in the igloo in our demon forms, Cam was keen on testing out the limits of his shapeshifting ability and the limits of what I could take in terms of size, stamina, and kink level. He'd shapeshift into one my favorite actors and surprise me in the living room, or shower, or bedroom . . . basically anywhere I was when the urge struck him.

I wasn't about to complain. You haven't lived until you've had countertop kitchen sex with massive-cocked Chris Hemsworth and Misha Collins lookalikes back to back. Penelope would lose her mind if she knew how many orgasms I'd had with her favorite, Castiel.

Unfortunately, the ridiculous amount of torrid sex we had didn't seem to lessen the annoying sense of danger I'd been feeling since our return. I just couldn't shake it. It was there when I woke and didn't go away until I went to sleep at night.

And, of course, Cam, being the martyr he was, blamed himself for it. Somehow, he had convinced himself that he was the cause, though I tried to explain over and over that it couldn't be him. Whoever I was feeling, they planned to do us harm. Cam would never hurt me. He loved me too much.

That explanation seemed to appease him for a while, but after forty-eight hours of watching his fiancée pace, worry, and rub her chest, he finally asked, "Mavis, really, darling. Don't you think it could be me?"

"No," I told him, stopping my pacing to curl up on the couch in his arms. "I've already told you. This just started while we were on the mountain, and it amplifies at weird intervals. If it were you, wouldn't it be stronger when I'm near you?"

"Maybe," he said, stroking the side of my face. "But you can't deny that all of this started the night I showed you my demon form. That seems like too much of a coincidence."

I shook my head. "That may be true, but you have to

remember, it started after Penelope woke me. You'd been in your demon form for hours before I first felt it. It can't be you." I bit my lip, going over the events of that night. "I'm starting to think it might have been someone working for your father," I admitted.

Cameron frowned and hugged me tighter to his body. "That is not what I want to hear six hours before I leave town, Mavis."

"Trust me. I don't want it to be true either, but what else could it be?"

"Could the throttle Severin had placed around your heart be completely broken now? Maybe you're just feeling this because of all of the other demons in town?"

I sighed. "I do feel like this has something to do with my Exitium Daemonium thing, but I don't think this feeling would wax and wane like it's doing if it wasn't a specific demon doing something nefarious. It's almost as if I'm sensing their evil intent or something. Sometimes it's strong. Sometimes it's not."

"So, you think your Exitium Daemonium magic is sort of like a douche radar?"

I lifted my head from his chest and met his eyes. "That's exactly what I'm thinking."

"And you're sure it's not me?"

"Are you doing something douchey or evil?" I asked, smirking at him.

Cam grimaced and stared out the window at the snowfall before answering. "Sometimes my control over my urges slips and the need to steal souls is overwhelming. I'm trying to figure out a way to conquer those feelings, but I can't seem to do it without a sexual release."

"Is that why we've been having so much sex lately?"

Cam slid his hands down to cup my ass and said, "No, we have so much sex because you're the hottest demon I've ever had my dick in."

I narrowed my eyes at him. "How many demon chicks have you had your dick in?"

He pursed his full lips, looking like he wished he'd never said anything. "No comment."

"That many, huh?" I asked, laughing at his expression.

"Let's just say it's more than a handful and leave it at that, okay?"

"Oh, it's definitely more than a handful," I said, trying to take his mind off his worry by tracing the outline of his growing erection through his pajama pants. "Way more than a handful."

"I think that's just hearsay unless you prove it," he said, his voice thick with lust.

"Is that right?" I asked, tugging down the waistband of his pajamas to expose the hard length of him.

"Yeah, it's science or something."

I smiled and wrapped both hands around his cock, using them both to stroke him. "I was right. You do have more than a handful."

He groaned, letting his head fall back. "What do you intend on doing with this knowledge?"

"I don't really know," I told him, sliding down to my knees in front of him. "I think we might have to do a little more research. Maybe see if it's more than a mouthful. You know, for science's sake."

He lifted his head and ran a thumb over my bottom lip. "I guess you better find out. I wouldn't want to stand in the way of your pursuit of knowledge."

"How magnanimous of you," I said, running my tongue from base to tip.

Cam leaned forward to rid me of my short nightgown, leaving me in only a pair of black lace panties. "I do what I can, little demon."

I gave him a sensual smile and said, "Let's see what I can do," before enveloping his cock with my mouth as far as it would go.

"Fuck!" he barked out, bucking his hips.

Letting him slide almost all the way out, I swirled my tongue around the head, then fully took him in my mouth again. He moaned and wrapped my ponytail around his hand, yanking me away so he could stand. I stared up at him hungrily. "Fuck my mouth, Cam."

He didn't waste a second complying with my wishes. Forcing his way past my lips, he held my head still as he pumped his cock into my mouth, hard and fast. My jaw ached, and my scalp hurt from his firm grip on my hair, but I didn't care. I wanted to please him. I wanted his cum down my throat. I wanted him to use me however he wanted, come wherever he wanted, then I wanted him to fuck me until I couldn't take it anymore.

"Fuck, you're beautiful," Cam growled. "I love the way you look with my cock sliding in and out of that perfect little pouty mouth."

Unable to respond, I wrapped a hand around the base of him and cupped his balls with the other, all while staring up at him with ravenous eyes. I wanted him to know how much I liked this, how wet it made me just to taste him.

He groaned loudly as his body transformed into his demon shape, and his cock grew bigger, stretching my aching jaw to a painful level. I knew he would come soon, and I wanted it, craved it.

Panting for breath, he roared as he slipped from my lips, covering my face and breasts with his cum before shoving himself back into my mouth to finish himself off.

I whimpered, desperate for him to give me the same release, the same extreme pleasure.

He didn't disappoint. Without missing a beat, he pulled his slick cock out of my mouth and gingerly guided me by the hair until I was positioned over the arm of the couch. "Beg me to come inside of you," he said, sliding two long fingers into my wetness. "Beg me to fill you up."

"Please," I pleaded, chasing the pleasure he was giving me with my hips. "Shove that big fucking cock into my pussy. Make me your whore. I want to feel your cum dripping down my thighs."

I knew he'd be shocked. I'd never said anything like that before, but I couldn't bring myself to care. I wanted everything I'd asked for and more.

His voice was dark, dangerous as he asked, "You want to be my whore, Mavis?"

"Yes," I replied, moaning as he removed his fingers and forced them into my mouth, so I could taste myself.

"You want this big dick in that tight little pussy?" he asked, guiding his massive cock to my opening and teasing me by only pushing the head in.

"Yes!" I cried out. "Give me more. I want all of you inside me."

He chuckled and cupped my breasts, pinching the nipples cruelly. "You like being my little slut, don't you?"

"Yes. Please, Cameron. Fuck me," I begged, unable to wait any longer. I felt like I would go out of my mind if he didn't let me come soon.

Finally relenting, he slid in to the hilt, making me cry out in pleasured pain. Moving his right hand from my breast to my clit, he asked, "Is this dick what you wanted?"

"Yes," I said, nearly sobbing with relief. "Fuck, I love the feel of you filling me up."

"Do I make you want to come on this big cock?" he asked, working my clit at the same fast rhythm he was fucking me.

"Harder!" I screamed, rocking my body against him as the orgasm I'd so desperately wanted hit me all at once.

"That's it," he hissed into my ear. "Milk my cock, Mavis. Make me come in that tight little pussy."

"Come in me," I growled out, already close to another orgasm. "Make me take it all."

Yanking my head back by my ponytail, he pulled me flush

against his chest and pinned me there as he pounded into me over and over. "Come," he ordered. "Make that pussy come again."

He didn't have to ask me twice. I howled out my release loudly, riding out wave after wave of pain mixed with throbbing, exquisite pleasure.

He followed right after, yelling, "Fuck!" as he pumped harder and harder into me, finally collapsing, spent, breathless, and satisfied, on top of my sweat-covered body.

We stayed that way for a few minutes, catching our breaths, before I sighed and asked, "Are you sure you have to go out of town tonight?"

"I'm not sure I can move," he said, chuckling in my ear. "I was going to make you dinner before I left, but now I'm thinking you should call Penny and ask her to bring you Chinese on her way home from work."

"Deal," I agreed. "And I will . . . as soon as I can walk."

CHAPTER 8

*P*enelope got home from her shift at Sakura Buffet in record time. As soon as she came in the door, she threw the little paper containers of food she'd brought home on the coffee table and ran to plop down onto the carpet in front of the TV, eager to catch every second of the *Supernatural* episode starting in two minutes.

"Hey, stranger. It's nice to see you, too," I said, laughing at her theatrics from the couch.

"Yeah, yeah," she said, not looking away from the screen. "Less talky. More watchy."

"Oh no," I told her, grabbing the remote. "We will be talking about the fact that I haven't seen you or Ray in more than forty-eight hours."

She frowned at me. "Ray hasn't been home for two days?"

I shook my head. "Nope. I figured you guys might be finishing the little tête-à-tête you started on the mountain."

She snorted. "Tête-à-tête? No. I worked back-to-back double shifts just to keep myself from taking him up on the facial he offered. I haven't seen him since we all had lunch at Napoli's."

I sat up, alarmed. "So he's missing? Why does this stuff always happen when Cam is out of town?"

"What stuff?" Ray asked, coming out of his room with a fluffy blue towel wrapped around his hips and nothing else.

"What the fuck, Ray?" I asked, pinching the bridge of my nose. "I thought you were gone, or, at the very least, clothed."

He shrugged. "I got home this morning while you and Cam were getting it on in the shower. I didn't think you'd want me to interrupt your multiple orgasms to tell you I was here, so I just went to bed."

I glared at him. "I have told you that you can knock, right?"

"Yes, you have," he said, grinning. "Now be quiet so Penny and I can watch Castiel get his ass kicked by the thing from the Empty."

"Really? You're going to sit on my couch in a towel and watch *Supernatural?*"

Penelope huffed. "Mavis, you're missing this touching moment with Jack and his mom. Either shut it, or I'm shoving an egg roll down your throat."

"*Supernatural* makes you violent," I complained, getting up to go to the kitchen.

"Sticks and stones, babe," she retorted, turning back to the TV.

"She doesn't get it," Ray said, bending down to kiss her on the cheek. "She's too caught up in her own supernatural drama."

"Says the demon who's wearing a towel instead of pants," I said, coming out of the kitchen with plates and forks.

He flashed a grin in my direction and said, "Mavis, if I don't do things like this, how else am I going to show Penny what she's missing?"

"I've seen what I'm missing," Penelope said, not taking her eyes off the TV. "I don't suppose you can make it whatever size you want like Cam, can you?"

Clearly insulted, he said, "No, but I promise you that I've never had any complaints about my size before."

"Yeah, well, I don't want to have to go get a designer vagina because you've massacred it with your giant dick."

I stopped spooning the fragrant Kung Pao chicken onto the plates and had to brace myself on the coffee table to keep from laughing at Ray's dumbstruck face. "Penelope, I think you broke him."

Clearing his throat, he stood up, careful to keep said dick out of our eyesight. "I think I'm going to take that shower now."

"Don't you want to eat first?" I asked, holding up his plate.

"Later, Mavis," he said, rushing down the hall to the guest bathroom. "I've got to . . ."

"Masturbate in the shower while you think about massacring Penelope's vagina?" I suggested.

"Something like that, yeah," he admitted. "Sorry, ladies."

"It's not your fault you were born with a massive cock," Penelope called after him.

She looked at me with mischief twinkling in her eyes and laughed when she heard him groan as he shut the door.

I shook my head and handed her a plate. "That demon is whipped. I would tell you to throw him a bone, but . . ." I motioned to the bathroom. "I think he's got his own."

Ray finally reappeared from the bathroom a few minutes after Penelope went home to take her own shower and get ready for bed. She'd wanted to wait him out, but after *Supernatural*, she was dozing off on the couch. Part of me thought that working herself too hard to avoid Ray was silly since they were pretty much an item at this point, but the other part of me was glad she wasn't spending too much time with him, especially when he came out of the bathroom bare-chested with a pair of tight, frayed Levi's on, looking every bit like the kind of male that would fuck her, break her heart, and disappear.

"You're wasting your time with that sexy *look at me* thing you've got going on," I said, digging into a pint of Cherry Garcia. "She's gone."

"Is this the part where you threaten me for having designs on your friend?" he asked, sitting in the chair across from me and lacing his fingers across his tanned, muscled abs.

I stuck the spoon into the ice cream and squinted at him. "No, this is the part where I tell you that if you hurt her, I will hunt you to the ends of the earth and make you wish you were dead."

Unfazed, his expression didn't change. "You can cool your jets, Mavis. I don't want to hurt her. I actually really like her. She's prickly and sexy, and sarcastic—all the things I like in a woman."

"She's also human," I pointed out. "A human that Cam and I love very much. I don't want her getting mixed up with any clandestine demon shit you've got going on, on the outside."

"Says the demon that hangs out with her, knowing that she could end up being collateral damage in this whole Exitium Daemonium thing with Severin," he said, a note of accusation in his voice. "Aren't you the least bit concerned that he could use her as leverage to get what he wants?"

"Of course I'm concerned," I retorted, setting the ice cream down on the coffee table a little harder than I intended. "I would never involve her with anything regarding Severin . . . ever. Especially since Cameron's father has always pressured him to take her soul."

"He what?" he demanded, his hands practically strangling the arms of the chair as he sat up straight.

Stunned at the intensity in his voice, I stared at him, wondering what was going through his mind. He'd worked for Severin before. He had to know what kind of sick fuck he could be, and he had to know what he was capable of. Why was this such a shock to him?

"Cam told me that he's been trying to pressure him into stealing Penelope's soul ever since she met him," I reiterated.

"Do you know when the last time Severin saw her with Cam was?"

I shook my head. "Not a clue. I only met him once before our showdown on Mount Sousa."

He nodded and ran his hand through his hair, making it stand up on end. "Do you think Penelope would temporarily move in here with us until after things get resolved between you and Severin?"

I laughed. "Penelope? No. Not unless you do some major convincing. If you haven't noticed, she's pretty fucking independent."

He frowned. "That I have."

"So, what now?" I asked, offering him some of my ice cream. "What do you think we should do?"

He dug out a huge spoonful and shrugged. "Short of hiring a guard armed with some sort of demon-killing artifact to follow her around twenty-four seven, I have no idea. Are you still getting the weird vibes?"

I furrowed my brow. "Not tonight, which is actually kind of strange. The vibrations have been constant while you were gone."

He nodded again, lost in thought as he chewed.

"What are you thinking?" I asked, hoping he wasn't planning something crazy.

"I don't know what to think," he said, getting up and starting to pace as he dug out another spoonful. "If Severin wants her, what can we do? You said he wasn't affected by your demon-killing powers, right?"

"Yeah, he laughed when it didn't work and said, 'Who do you think had the throttle put in your chest,' or something to that effect."

Ray handed the container back to me and continued his pacing.

"Will the powers that be in Havenwood Falls force her to leave for her own good?"

"I honestly don't know why they would. This is the safest place in the world. Where could we take her that would be safer than here?"

He stopped suddenly and sat back down, looking completely hopeless. "I can't lose her, Mavis. I love her. We have to do something to keep her safe."

I smiled at his honesty. "I think she might feel the same for you. Although, seriously, you two have the weirdest way of showing your affection."

"I think that's why I like her so much," he said, a smile playing at his lips. "She doesn't put up with any of my bullshit, and she doesn't fall all over herself trying to impress me like the demon females do."

"I'm thinking a lot of demon females do that, don't they?"

He winked at me, perking up. "More than you'd think. I'm nearly irresistible."

"You and Cam have that in common."

He chuckled. "Yeah, but I've been doing it with only God-given hotness. Cam's magic draws females to him."

"I see modesty is also something you two have in common," I said, rolling my eyes toward the heavens.

Ray smirked, then gave me a wry smile. "Who needs modesty when you look like this?"

CHAPTER 9

I was sleeping when Cameron came home in a blind panic late the next morning. He rushed into the apartment, slinging the door open wide, screamed out my name, then nearly cried in relief when I stumbled sleepily out of the bedroom and met him in the hall.

"What's going on?" I asked, leaning heavily against the wall, when a wave of hostile intent crashed over me.

"Thank God" was all Cam said as he pulled me into his embrace, holding me tight against his body. "I thought . . . I thought he'd gotten to you."

"Who?" I asked, pulling away to look into his worried brown eyes.

"Rayonus," he spat.

Confused, I asked, "Rayonus? What do you mean? He was just here last night."

A look of rage filled his features as what I said sank in. "When was the last time you saw him, Mavis? When?"

I stared at him, shocked. I'd never seen him angry like this before. "I don't know. It couldn't have been later than nine o'clock. He showed up right after Penelope brought dinner."

"Penelope!" he exclaimed, running to the door. "Wait there. Right there. Don't move."

I wrapped my arms around myself, scared of what was coming next. I knew he wouldn't find Penelope there. I knew she would be gone, and from the sound of it, Rayonus had taken her. But why? What was happening?

Cam ran back into the apartment, breathless and forlorn. "She's gone, Mavis," he said, his voice cracking as he grabbed me and buried his face in my hair. "She's gone, and I don't know where to look for her."

"Baby, tell me what's happening," I said, stroking his back and trying to comfort him as best as I could.

"Rayonus," he said when he finally found his voice. "He and my father . . ."

"They were working together," I guessed, knowing the answer before he even said it. "That motherfucker."

He nodded. "I ran into an old acquaintance working at a gas station in Denver. She told me that she'd seen Severin and Rayonus in Grand Junction not a week ago."

"Why didn't she call you to let you know?" I asked with unshed tears in my eyes.

He cupped my face in his hands. "She doesn't know about our situation. If I told her I'm marrying the Exitium Daemonium, we'd have every would-be evil overlord in the world trying to figure out how to get into Havenwood Falls."

I raised my brows. "So, she's a trustworthy old friend."

Cam almost smiled. "Actually, yes. But Mavis, you're the Exitium Daemonium. No one else can know about you. Even abnormally nice demons are still demons. There's always a little evil lurking within us. You can't trust us."

I sighed, in complete disbelief over what was about to come out of my mouth. "Cameron, I know you think that, but in Rayonus's case, I don't think you have anything to worry about. At least, not where Penelope is concerned."

Incredulous, he dropped his hands and stepped away from me. "How could you know that?"

"Because when he was here last night, he kind of freaked out. He told me he loved her and wanted to get her out of town, or at the least, to move in here with us where she could be watched. Now that this has happened, I'm guessing he knew she was about to be used to blackmail us into coming to Severin, and he decided to get her out of town."

"Or my father told him to take her," he argued. "There's no way to know for sure."

"Not until we talk to Ray, no," I said, thinking aloud as I stared at the carpet. "And either way, I'm sure he's doing what he thought was safest for her. He's been loyal to you out of friendship, but he loves her. I have a feeling if it came down to it, he would do anything to keep her from getting hurt, even if that meant he would have to betray us."

"Mavis, you said you were feeling your douche radar when I left yesterday. Did it get worse or better when he was here?"

"Neither. It disappeared."

I looked up to see a glimmer of hope in his eyes. "It disappeared?" he asked.

I shrugged. "Yeah, a few hours after you left."

Cam sighed in relief, closing his eyes. "Mavis, this is good news."

Astonished, I asked, "It is? How?"

"You weren't feeling any negative intent from him," he explained, leading me to the couch to sit. "He didn't set off your radar."

"That's good, I guess, but that still doesn't leave us with any way to find her. Or to kick his ass from here to next Tuesday. Because, right now, I don't give a shit whether his intentions were good. His ass is grass when I get ahold of him. She wouldn't even be in this mess if he didn't come here to try to buddy up to us for your father."

"I know," he said, pulling me into a hug. "And I know you want to kick his ass, but I want you to promise me you'll dial back that demon-killing urge until we know the whole truth, okay?"

I pushed away from him, knowing he was right, but not wanting to listen. I just wanted Penelope back, safe and sound in Havenwood Falls, where she belonged.

"Look," he said, trying to get me to see reason. "Rayonus has a place about an hour and a half from here, up near Montrose. We'll drive up there and see if they're there. If they're not, we'll assume he's joined the dark side, and we'll figure out our next step."

"Don't you think we should call Sheriff Kasun and report this?"

He shook his head. "No, his jurisdiction doesn't go any farther than the county limits. Plus, I just don't want him getting caught in the crosshairs of some demon fight he can't handle."

Taking a deep breath to steel myself, I stood. "Okay, I'll get dressed, and we'll go."

Cam and I drove out of Havenwood Falls in silence, both of us with thoughts weighing heavy on our minds. I so wanted to agree with Cam and think the best of Rayonus. I really did; he had seemed so sincere about his worry for Penelope the night before, but when I thought back to all the lies and deceptive things he'd done, the secrecy he'd always kept himself shrouded in, I didn't know if I believed he could be on our side. I kept thinking back to his words in the outdoors store when he said that not all demons have the capacity for good that Cameron does.

Those words hadn't meant much then, but they were glaringly

accurate to me now. As far as I was concerned, I'd never met and would never meet a demon that had the capacity for good Cam did, because they were never human. His humanity—that goodness his mom had given him—was what made him the decent male I wanted to marry, that I wanted to be with for an eternity. Ray had never had that, and he never would.

Cam had been driving for thirty or forty minutes when he bit out a sudden, alarmed curse and said, "I think we're in trouble, darling."

"What is it?" I asked, squinting ahead at the metallic shimmer blocking the road in the distance.

"If I had to take a guess, I'd say it's my father and his cohorts. There are another two cars behind us as well."

"Fuck!" I exclaimed, whipping around in my seat to see that there were, in fact, two dark-windowed black sedans following closely behind us. "What do we do?"

He reached across the console and squeezed my hand. "Protect yourself as best as you can. If we get taken and something happens to me, try to find Penelope. If you can find her, get yourselves out and away however you can."

Fat tears rolled down my cheeks. "Cam, you're scaring me."

He lifted my hand to his mouth, kissed it, then wiggled the engagement ring loose. "Hide this in between the seats. My father will torture me to get you to agree to his wishes. Don't give him any more leverage than he already has."

Nodding woodenly, I quickly grabbed a receipt from the dash, balled the ring up in it, and shoved it between the console and the passenger seat. "Now what?"

He gripped the steering wheel tightly and stared ahead at what we could see were two black SUVs parked across the lanes. "We try to go around them if there's room, or we go through the middle. Is your seatbelt buckled tight?"

I jerked on the shoulder strap, cinching it tighter to my hips. "Yes."

"Then hold on, darling," he said, gunning the accelerator. "I'm bringing us up to ramming speed."

Blowing out a deep breath, I closed my eyes and prayed that we'd make it, prayed that we'd get out of this with our lives, prayed that Penelope was okay, and prayed that I would never get ahold of Ray because I was going to kill him.

"Hold on!" Cam yelled as we slammed into the middle of the SUVs.

The deafening screech of metal against metal drowned out my screams as our SUV plowed through, pushing the two cars to a diagonal position on either side of us. We sped ahead for a few beats, and for a second, I thought we'd made it, but then the front driver's side tire blew, leaving us skidding across the road and into the snow-filled ditch.

"Run!" Cam screamed as soon as our momentum stopped. "Run as fast as you can! I'm right behind you."

Dazed, I threw the seatbelt off me and opened the door, ready to dash up the mountain to the safety of the trees. I knew they'd easily catch up to me if I ran down the highway. I'd only gotten a few steps from the car when electricity, so white-hot it blinded me, shot through my body. I stumbled, falling to my knees, but still tried to crawl to the tree line. In my addled mind, I thought if I could make it to the trees, I'd be safe. If I could make it to the trees, this would be over. And then everything went black.

CHAPTER 10

The first thing I saw when I woke was blackness. Panicked, I tried to sit up from my prone position on what felt like concrete and was rewarded with a cruel laugh for my trouble.

"Don't even try it," a male voice said. "Severin's not letting you go anywhere."

I feigned ignorance. "Who? I don't understand what's going on."

Cue another annoying laugh. "Sure you don't."

"Stop toying with her, Felix," another voice said. "Severin has been looking for you."

This voice I knew. It was Rayonus. The backstabbing, lying asshole who had betrayed us.

"Mavis?" he inquired, gingerly lifting the blindfold from my eyes.

"Evil henchman," I retorted coldly as I blinked the black-haired demon into focus.

"I deserve that," he said, giving me a significant look that I didn't understand. "You must be pissed that I lied to you."

"Pissed?" I seethed. "Pissed? I don't think 'pissed' really covers it, do you?"

He grimaced and said, "No," but then mouthed out, "Cam is okay."

I glanced around the small eight-by-ten cell I was in. There was nothing in it—not a bed, chair, or toilet—and it smelled like mildew and mold. "Where's Penelope? What did you do with her?"

"I'll answer that if you don't mind," Severin said, walking into the small cell, looking like a model on the cover of a romance novel. "We haven't had a chance to talk for a few months."

Ray bowed. "Yes, Lord Severin."

"Aw . . . is someone having an identity crisis?" I asked, taunting my incubus douchebag soon-to-be father-in-law.

Closing the door behind Rayonus, he hissed, "Shut your mouth, ice demon."

I laughed shrilly. "Or what? You'll tell your mommy on me?"

Severin dragged me from the ground by my hair and squeezed my chin painfully in his grip as he hovered over me. "I said to shut up, Mavis."

Scoffing, I spit in his face. "Go fuck yourself, demon boy."

Chuckling darkly, Severin wiped the spit from his face with his hand and licked it. "Breaking you is going to give me so much pleasure. When I'm done with you—"

"I'm going to ask if you've put it in yet. Yeah, that's sad, Severin. That's not the kind of thing you should tell folks either. Lest they pity your poor impotent ass."

He bared his fangs at me and shoved me away, turning to leave, then, second-guessing his decision, he backhanded me so hard I fell to the floor.

The rough concrete dug painfully into my hands and knees as I landed, and the room spun around me. I scrambled back to my feet, swaying but ready to take him on. "Is that all you got, Severin?"

"No," he said coldly. "But sadly, as much pleasure as it brings me to see you bleeding, I have more important things to attend to." He grinned down at me, his black eyes roaming over my body as he adjusted his growing erection.

"I'm going to kill you, Severin DeSalle," I said, ambling toward him through the pain. "I'm going to kill you and rejoice in the sound of your screams."

His voice was hard and unforgiving as he turned away from me, not even remotely afraid of what I might do. "You do that," he said. "If you think you can."

"I can!" I yelled, slinging an icicle at the door as it closed behind him. "And I will!"

His taunting laugh echoed in the hallway before he called, "Put my son in here with her," to the guard outside the cell. "And make sure he knows the weight of my displeasure with him when you do."

~

Rayonus returned as soon as Severin left. He was carrying a bowl of water, a washcloth, and a worried expression. "You're bleeding, Mavis. You have a bad cut on your cheek."

I reached up to the cheek Severin had just struck and hissed in pain. "You are all going to pay for this," I told him, my voice as frigid and unfeeling as the ice in my veins. "I'm going to kill every single last one of you."

Ray winced, knowing I meant every word. "I know, and I don't blame you," he whispered. "But before you do, let me get you three out of here."

"How?" I asked skeptically, not believing him for a second.

He shook his head. "I don't know, but I will. I promised you once that I didn't mean you any harm. That hasn't changed. I never wanted any of this to happen."

"He has us both. Why doesn't he let Penelope go now?"

He gave me a bitter smile and squeezed out the cloth. "I love her. He knows I'll do anything he says to keep her safe."

I let out a little sob as what little hope I had that Penelope would get out of this alive left me. "Can I see her?"

"Eventually," he told me, his jaw clenching and unclenching in anger as he looked over my wounded hands. "But I'm sure Severin will want to try to get you in line before he rewards you."

Tears sprang into my eyes. "I hate you, Ray."

Dabbing at the drying blood on my cheek, he nodded. "I hate myself."

"Good."

For what seemed like an eternity, I waited for Severin to keep his promise of sending Cam to me bloody. I didn't doubt his threats and bitterly regretted antagonizing him into doing it, even though Ray assured me he would heal quickly. I knew he was right— demons did heal incredibly fast—but I still asked him to leave the bowl of water and the cloth just in case I needed it.

Finally, after I'd paced around the four-walled cell a hundred times, I heard the snick of the lock. I ran forward, careful to keep my distance from the actual door, and prayed I'd see Cam walk in on his own two feet.

No such luck.

Cam was battered and bruised on every inch of his body. His dark hair had been torn out in patches. His eyes were so swollen, he couldn't open them. Bloody tears leaked between the lids. But he was alive and mad enough to call out anatomically impossible threats to the goons that brought him in before they left.

I waited until they closed the door to rush to his side. "Cam," I said, whispering so low, I hoped he could hear me.

Mavis," he sighed out, another bloody tear leaking down his face. "Darling, I'm so sorry. If I would have known they were going to ambush us—"

"Shhh," I said, gently wiping his cheeks with the cloth. "It's okay. I'm okay. Penelope's okay, too. Ray said she's in the basement."

"Thank God," he breathed. "Do you know where we're at?"

"No, I think they tased me. The last thing I remember is running and feeling a searing pain in my chest. I woke up blindfolded in this cell."

He was silent for a moment before he asked, "And my father? Have you seen him?"

"He was here about thirty minutes ago. I'm afraid I might have caused your injuries by smarting off to him. I'm so sorry."

Cameron smiled, though it looked like it pained him. "You? Smart off to someone? Never."

"How can you make jokes right now?" I asked, sniffing and wiping my tears from my cheeks with the back of my hand.

He pushed himself slowly to a sitting position. "This isn't the first time my father has had me beaten. It won't be the last."

"You can't take any more, Cam. If you could see what I'm seeing, you'd understand. It's bad, Cam."

"We're demons," he said, smiling ruefully. "That's the beauty of it to him. It used to take days for me to heal, but now, I can already feel my ribs knitting themselves back together. He'll be able to do this again within the next couple of hours."

Horrified, I asked, "He did this to you before, when you were half human?"

"He's done it a thousand times, Mavis. Why do you think I was so keen to keep stealing souls for him? Angering him wasn't worth the weekly beatings."

I stared at Cam, trying to center my emotions through the rusty smell of his blood, the torrent of vibrations in my chest, and the homicidal urge that shot through me when I focused on his bruised and beaten face. "I'm so sorry you were born into this life," I told him, meaning every word with all my heart. "If I can stop this, if I can snuff him out, I will."

"It could be worse," he said, trying to open his eyes. "If he had demanded that I stay in his entourage of lackeys, this would happen much more regularly, and I would've never met you."

"Well, that may not be exactly true. If we hadn't met on the road that night, he'd probably have me as one of his lackeys by now."

His square jaw hardened as he clenched his teeth against the pain and stood up to take a look at our surroundings. "That will never happen," he said firmly. "I won't let it."

"You may not have a choice, Cam. I mean, seriously, how are we going to get out of here? If I can't fight against him, we're going to need help."

Turning to me, he gathered me into his arms and hugged me tightly. "It may take time," he whispered. "We may have to do things we never thought possible. But Mavis, one day, he will slip up. One day, we'll overtake him. And on that day, you will kill him."

I knew he was right. This was a bad situation, a terrible one, but it wasn't an impossible situation. We were immortal. We could wait Severin out. In time, he would make a mistake, and we would be ready.

"Isn't this sweet," Severin said, walking into the cell. "The two lovebirds are reunited."

Cam and I remained silent as he closed the door behind him and casually leaned against the wall. "What?" he asked. "No biting wit or comments, ice demon? No more threats or spitting in my face? I thought you were going to—what was it—rejoice in the sound of my screams?"

A scathing reply was on the tip of my tongue, but I held it back when Cameron gave my arm a nearly imperceptible squeeze, letting the hatred in my eyes say everything I couldn't.

Severin chuckled. "I thought seeing this embarrassment of an incubus beaten and broken would change your mind. You lesser demons are so fucking predictable."

"Father, allow me to—"

"Quiet!" Severin bellowed. "I've heard quite enough from you two today. As a matter of fact, I like the calm your lover has when she sees you like this. It seems to make that feral attitude she has a bit more docile."

I glared at him, biting my cheek so hard I could taste blood welling into my mouth.

Severin crossed the room to stand in front of me. "You want to hurt me, don't you, you little hellcat? You want to grind me into a spot on the ground like you did your poor grandfather, don't you?"

I didn't answer, but I didn't cower, either. I just stared up at him, memorizing every line on his face, every hair on his head. I wanted to remember it all because when I killed him —and I would —he would be nothing. He would be less than nothing. There would be no way to recognize him when I was done.

Stroking a hand down my cheek, Severin smiled. "I can see the burning desire in you, Mavis. I can practically feel the heat of your anger, the depth of your hatred. I can't help but wonder, if I made you my lover, would you still have that fire behind your eyes or would you cower in fear like the rest of the demons do when they see my cock?"

Disgusted, I sneered at him. "Fuck you, Severin."

The corners of his mouth lifted in a half smile. "Oh, little demon, you think this bastard son of mine has brought you pleasure? You have no idea the pain, the degradation that you would enjoy with me. You would beg me for it. Do anything for it. They all do . . . after a little persuasion."

Severin glanced at his son's defiant face and sneered.

"Relinquish her to me, Cameron, and I'll free you and your human friend. Give me my prize, and I will let you walk away from this life."

Cameron shook his head, though he knew the consequences of refusing his father. "No."

Severin's voice was deceptively calm as he asked, "You dare to defy me?"

"She is *my* prize," Cam told him. "My destiny. Taint her with your evil if you will, but she will always be mine."

"Foolish words from a foolish demon," his father retorted, dragging me from his son's arms and throwing me against the wall.

The breath flew from my chest as I hit the concrete, but I righted myself quickly. I would stand and fight him, no matter if it was with my last dying breath. I wouldn't just roll over and let him win.

"When will you both understand that I am lord here?" Severin screamed, his face distorted with unbridled rage. "I make the rules! I care nothing for your sentiments and bravery! You will bend to my will!"

Then like someone flipped a switch, he calmed, turned to me, and gave me a serene smile. "I enjoy seeing that righteous light die in your eyes. I revel in it, just like you will, Exitium Daemonium. Oh, sure, you'll fight me now, but there will come a time very soon that you'll crave the destruction I want, and you'll do anything I ask to get it."

Stalking to where I stood, Severin grabbed my face with both hands and tilted it up. His black eyes swam with a sea of swirling souls, twisting, turning, yearning to break out of their prison. I tried to shrink away from the horror in those eyes, the clear intent in his movements, but he held fast.

"You already know what's to come, don't you? Your power—it can feel them, can't it?" He shook his head in wonder. "You will be magnificent," he said, before brushing his lips against mine.

I stiffened and tried to pull away, but he held me in place, pushing the soul into my mouth until I couldn't breathe. Helplessly, I tried to fight against him, scratching, punching, and kicking anything within my reach until whatever hold he had on me evaporated. I was left standing, cold and shaking, as he swept from the room without another glance.

CHAPTER 11

hen the shock of what Severin had done wore off, an overwhelming sense of fear, love, hate, betrayal, and anger struck me all at once. Nearly doubling over with the emotions, I asked, "What is this, Cam?"

His voice was even and without emotion as he answered, "Humanity."

I jerked my gaze to his face. "It feels . . . I've never felt like this before. It's so . . . much."

He nodded, understanding exactly how it felt to have a soul. He'd had his own only five and a half short months ago.

"Why did he do this?"

Cameron laughed, but there was no mirth in it, no joy. "I'm an incubus, Mavis. You know what we do."

"But what purpose could it have? What's his game?"

Cam closed his eyes and breathed out slowly as he shook his head. "He wants me to take it. He knows that we won't be able to resist each other."

Confused, I said, "I still don't get it, Cam. Why would he give a demon a soul?"

"To weaken me. Well, to be more precise, to weaken both of us."

"Me, I get. But how would stealing a soul weaken you?"

"It's my soul that he gave you."

My mouth dropped open. "Your soul? But how?"

"My father is well-known for his . . . let's call them talents. He can collect the souls of half demons, but they are no use to the powers that be above him; demons are already creatures of hell, so he saves them and uses them to strengthen himself.

"Then why would he voluntarily give yours to me?" I asked, still not quite understanding.

"With my soul inside of you, you won't have the amount of power you had before, just like I didn't have my full incubus powers. It'll be like before the throttle in your chest broke open. And if I steal it—which, let's face it, I will—these injuries that have healed in minutes might take days to heal. He doesn't like that I'm stronger as a demon. I can't be properly punished like this. I heal too quickly for his tastes."

"So, this is a really bad thing."

"A horrible thing," he agreed. "He knows that if he leaves us in here long enough together, one of us will lose control. You won't be able to resist me, and I won't be able to withstand your soul. Do you remember what it was like the first night we stayed together at that hotel?

I thought back to that night and the cringe-inducing way I'd acted without even realizing I was doing it. "Yes. I believe I tackled you like a 'sexed up cheetah' if I recall correctly.

He smiled at the memory, despite our shitty situation. "That you did."

I shook my head. "Cameron, what are we going to do?"

He pursed his lips. "I think we should have sex . . . eventually."

"But if you take your soul, you'll be defenseless."

"That's true, but you won't. You're the Exitium Daemonium.

You're the only one who can kill him. We just need to figure out a way to remove his talisman to make him vulnerable."

"How are we going to do that? We're locked in this cage."

"We won't be in here forever. This is just a temporary cell. He'll have to move us somewhere else. I'm guessing to his mansion in Grand Junction. That's where my father keeps all his prisoners."

With my mind still reeling from all the new emotions, I sank to the floor and wrapped my arms around my knees. "I know you're probably right about his motives, but I'm still worried that he might decide to separate us."

"He won't. He could have given you any number of souls, but he gave you mine. There's only one reason he'd do that."

I shuddered, thinking of all the souls I'd seen in his black eyes. "Why is he like this?"

Cam shed his jacket, handed it to me, then sighed. "Have you ever heard the phrase 'mad with power'?"

An hour or so after my soul transplant, Rayonus woke Cameron and me where we'd curled up together in a corner. We'd tried to stay apart, not wanting to risk the temptation we were already feeling, but without my ice magic, it was bitterly cold in the empty concrete cell, and my teeth chattering was getting bad enough that Cam had worried about me cracking a tooth that might not grow back.

"Severin wants you both moved downstairs with Penelope," he said, to both of our relief. As fiery as her short temper could be and as brave as she was, Penelope would be consumed by terror by now.

"Where are we, Rayonus?" Cam asked his friend quietly. "Where is he keeping us?"

Ray frowned, but said, "In a rented house about fifty miles east of Havenwood Falls."

Cam's hopeful expression fell. "So, it's too far for them to run if we can get them out."

"Do you really think Penelope would be here if I could get her out?" he asked.

"I don't know," I snapped, my swirling emotions getting the better of me. "Would she? You are the reason she's here."

Cam laid a hand on my shoulder to calm me. "That's not helping, Mavis. Don't let anger cloud your judgment."

"I've never had a soul before, Cam. This is a lot harder than you made it look."

Ray stared at us, realizing what we were saying. "Severin gave Mavis a soul?"

"He gave her my soul," Cam explained. "He's buying time and clearly planning on taking out a few of his frustrations on me later."

Ray froze as if the implications of having an incubus locked in a room with his pseudo-girlfriend had just hit him.

Cam sucked in a breath, following his line of thought. "You have my word, Rayonus. I won't touch her."

"It's not you I'm worried about. You know how humans react to you when you're not in Havenwood Falls. I don't think your tattoo will work here."

"Trust me," I told him. "She's going to be too angry at you to think about sex."

"She's right," Cam agreed. "Just go in there and act like your normal charming self. She'll be so pissed that you're acting like that, there's no way she'll think about sex with me."

Ray nodded. "Okay, but Cam?"

"You don't have to worry," Cam promised. "If the urge is too much to bear, I'll fuck my own girlfriend. I know you love her."

"Can you tell her that?" he asked. "I'm pretty sure I don't have a chance in hell with her after all the shit that's happened today, and even if I did, I don't deserve her.

❧

The guard unlocked the cell door a few minutes later, allowing Ray to lead Cam and me down a white-walled hallway, past several closed doors, and down a set of narrow steps to the damp basement. Only lit by a few candles, it was dark and gloomy and smelled like wet dog, but, thankfully, it was warmer than the cell we'd been in and furnished with a room off to the side that apparently had a toilet in it. It would be a lot more comfortable than the concrete floor we'd been sleeping on before.

When Penelope saw us, she jumped to her feet and ran to hug the absolute hell out of me.

"Are you okay?" I asked, looking her over for obvious injuries. Her long brown hair was tangled, and her clothes were disheveled, but otherwise, she didn't look any worse for wear.

"I'm okay," she said, tears in her eyes, "What's going on?"

"I tried to tell her," Ray said. "But once she found out I was connected to Severin, she wouldn't listen to me."

I squinted at him. "Do you really blame her, Ray? You lied to all of us. You're lucky we're not kicking your ass right now."

"Speak for yourself," Penelope said, rearing back and punching Rayonus as hard as she could in the nose.

"Ow!" Ray yelled, holding his broken nose.

"Whoa," I said, grabbing her by the arm and dragging her to the dirty couch. "Calm down. A lot of stuff is going on that you need to know about."

"More important than sweet, sweet vengeance?" she asked, seething with rage.

"For once, yes." I turned back to Ray. "Go, before Severin realizes that you're taking too long. I don't want him to come anywhere near Penelope."

He nodded but didn't move a muscle. "Penny, I'm sorry. I really am. I never wanted any of this to happen."

She stared right through him as he apologized, not once acknowledging that he was speaking to her. She would not be swayed by offers of regret or remorse. She was more pissed than I'd ever seen her. And I'd seen her throw a chair when she didn't realize *Supernatural* was on winter break.

Cam finally spoke up. "Rayonus, she'll be fine. Clearly, she can handle a demon on her own."

Ray took the stairs two at a time, only stopping once to glance back at Penelope, then he shut the door and locked it from the outside.

Penelope shook out her bloody hand and flexed her fingers. "Can someone please fill in the human? I'm starting to get a little cabin fevery in here."

CHAPTER 12

With Rayonus gone, Penelope deflated, sinking onto the couch with tears filling her brown eyes until they spilled down her cheeks. "I loved him, Mavis. When he came to my apartment to ask me to blow off work to go to his house in Montrose, I was going to tell him. How could he do this to me—to us? We trusted him."

Cameron sat down in the farthest chair from us and sighed. "You know the kind of demon my father is."

"Yes, but what does that have to do with me? Why would he want Ray to kidnap me?"

"To keep us in line," Cam explained. "What else?"

"What does he mean, 'keep you in line'?" she asked me.

For a moment, I sat there in silence, not knowing what to say. Everything felt so hard and never-ending now that I had a soul. I just wanted to wake up tomorrow and find this was all a terrible dream.

"Mavis?" Cam asked, sounding concerned, though he didn't dare come closer to us.

"I'm fine," I said, wiping my eyes. "I'm just not used to this soul thing. That's all."

"Soul thing?" Penelope asked. "What soul thing? Someone needs to start at the beginning and tell me what the hell is going on."

Sighing, I sat down next to her. "When Cam got wind of Ray's involvement with his father, he came home. After he realized I was okay, he went to your apartment and found it empty. With no leads on where you might be, the only logical place was Ray's house in Montrose. We thought that he was probably going to try to sneak you out of Havenwood Falls under Severin's nose after we put two and two together."

"Two and two?" she asked.

"I wasn't feeling the weird vibe anymore. It disappeared before you came home with dinner, and after you left, Ray sort of had a breakdown. He told me he loved you and berated me for not taking more steps to keep you safe with the impending deadline coming up."

"So, he was trying to save me, not kidnap me? And he told you he loved me?"

"We think so, and yes, he did say he loved you. He's been helping us a little bit since we've been in here."

She blew out a heavy breath. "Okay, where does the soul thing come in?"

"After Severin's goons made us wreck our car and tased us, we were brought here. I was taken to a cell and Cam was . . ." I searched for a word that wouldn't scare Penelope.

"I was beaten with a lead pipe," Cam supplied, apparently not feeling the need to sugarcoat the situation like I did.

"But you've healed already?" she asked, amazed.

"I've told you before how much faster demons heal than half-demons and humans, yes?"

She nodded and shrugged. "Yeah, I just didn't expect it to be this fast." Frowning, she added, "I knew I should have kicked one of those goons in the nuts."

Cam smirked. "And that is why we're friends. You always know what to say to lighten the mood."

I shook my head at the two. I couldn't believe they were making jokes right now. "Anyway, Severin came in and did the compulsory evil overlord speech. I spat in his stupidly handsome face and got backhanded for my trouble."

"You neglected to tell me that part," Cam admonished.

"You looked like you'd been run over by several cars when you came in," I shot back. "I didn't want to upset you."

"Point taken," he said, holding up his hands in defeat. "Continue, please."

I smiled at him. "Thank you. So, as I was saying, Ray came in after that with a wet cloth to wash the blood from my face, and Cam showed up shortly after. We were alone for a few minutes before Severin made a reappearance and gave another trite, boring attempt at overlord douchebaggery. He kissed me and kind of pushed Cam's soul into my mouth."

Penelope looked from me to Cam. "One, ew to the kiss, and two, why would he do that?"

"I'm an incubus," he said, shrugging. "He knew I wouldn't be able to resist the siren song of a soul, much less my own, and once I have my soul back, I won't heal nearly as fast. He can keep me weak."

"Not to mention," I added, "now that I've got a soul, it's almost just like when my throttle was whole. I can't transform at all, and I'm sensitive to the cold again."

"But what about the demon-killing thing? Does it affect that?"

"I haven't tried that out. I didn't want to hurt Cam or Ray, and Severin still has his amulet or talisman, whatever that is."

"I think he's keeping her weak until he can make other, more permanent, arrangements for us somewhere farther away from Havenwood Falls," Cam added.

Penelope suddenly looked apprehensive. "Cam, does your tattoo still work?"

He pressed his lips together. "No. I'm sorry, Penny. But don't worry. I promise I won't touch you."

She blew out another breath, this one shaky. "What do we do now?"

"We wait," I told her, settling onto the couch and looping my arm into hers. "There's not much else we can do."

"Welp," she said, her voice bright. "Who's up for a game of Three Questions?"

The time we spent waiting on word from Rayonus was some of the scariest but also the most lust-filled moments of my life. After talking for a couple of hours, an exhausted Penelope curled up on the couch and dozed off, leaving Cam and me alone to speak softly to each other while we watched her sleep. I tried to ignore the pull of his incubus power, tried to keep my eyes away from him, but the allure was too great.

"Do you think we can trust Ray?" I asked, trying to take our minds off the elephant in the room. I'd been staring at his full lips with hunger like I'd never felt before.

"I do," he growled, his eyes black with the same hunger I felt. "I just don't know if I can trust myself. You, with a soul, are the most beautiful, most seductive thing I've ever seen."

A slow smile spread across my lips. "Now you know how I felt when we met, incubus."

"I seriously doubt you felt like this, Mavis. The pull to your soul is almost impossible to ignore. As is your incredible body. Knowing exactly how you taste and how you feel while I'm inside of you makes it that much harder."

I moved closer to where he sat, my heart pounding in my ears. "Harder, you say?"

"Mavis," he warned. "I don't think I can control myself if you do this. Please don't make me do something we'll both regret later."

My eyes traveled the length of his body, stopping on the outline of his huge denim-clad erection. "I think having that big cock of yours deep inside of me would make me forget any regrets I might have."

He groaned, shifting his hips. "Mavis, please. It's hard enough without the verbal foreplay."

I bit my lip. "I love it when you say the word *hard*."

"For the love of *Supernatural*, guys!" Penelope exclaimed, sitting up. "Can you keep it in your pants for two seconds, so I can sleep?"

"Sorry," Cam and I said in unison as the bolt on the door was slid back.

"It's just me," Ray said, appearing with a tray of sandwiches and water.

I, for one, couldn't have been happier to see him. After he'd come to my aid in the cell and my initial anger had faded, I didn't really think he would leave us out to dry, but there was the underlying worry that he would, or that he would be found out by Severin and punished accordingly. Even after everything he'd done, I didn't want to see another friend hurt or worse.

After distributing pre-packaged sandwiches and bottles of water, he sat on the third step of the stairs and stared at Penelope, who, of course, refused to glance in his direction. "Is everything going okay down here?" he asked.

Cam nodded and took a swig from his water bottle. "As good as can be expected. Have you figured anything out yet?"

"Actually, I think so."

"What?" I asked, sitting on the edge of the couch to catch every word of his quiet conversation.

"Severin mentioned something about moving you to a 'long-term solution' for your imprisonment later tonight when he didn't think I was listening. I think that if we plan things right, we can escape during that transition. He's already sent most of the demons back to wherever that is to get it ready."

"What about his amulet?" Cam asked. "Mavis can't touch him while he's wearing it."

"You mean this one?" Ray asked, holding up the small charm between his fingers.

Cam jumped up, a triumphant expression on his face as he took the small runed piece of ivory from his friend and pocketed it. "How did you get it?"

Ray smiled winsomely. "I convinced one of his lovers to switch it out while she and another demoness were . . . uh, servicing him."

"How did you talk them into doing that?"

Ray smiled. "Severin may be powerful, but he's also a selfish lover with zero redeemable qualities. The sooner we kill him, the sooner they'll be free to go back to the life they had before he took them as sex slaves. I always told him that his treatment of others and burned bridges within the demon community would come back to bite him in the ass."

"I could kiss you," I told him, getting up to hug him.

He wrapped me in his warm embrace and grinned down at me. "Why don't you save that for Cameron? It'll be a good start to you giving his soul back."

"That it would," Cam said, eyeing me with renewed interest.

"You guys go ahead," he said, nodding his head toward the bathroom. "You may not get another chance. I'll watch Penelope while you're busy, then I'll go secure a car that will get her back to Havenwood Falls while you guys do the deed with Severin."

"Doesn't this seem a little too good to be true?" Penelope asked skeptically. "I mean, we all get kidnapped by one of the most powerful shape-shifting demons in the world and Rayonus Rixa is the one who outsmarts him? Really?"

Ray's smile fell as her words cut into him. "Penny, I know it's hard for you to trust me right now. I've hurt you. I've lied and done terrible things, but I really do love you. Seeing you here in this dank basement, scared and alone, you have no idea what it's done to me. I'll admit, I'm a selfish creature. I've always been selfish, but that stopped today. It's time that I put someone else's wishes and safety ahead of my own, and that someone is you."

Unfazed by a speech that had brought tears to my eyes, Penelope asked, "Okay, if you are who you say you are, what did you put on the top of Mavis and Cam's Christmas tree in December?"

With palpable relief, he smiled and answered, "Your favorite angel, Castiel, of course."

"That's good enough for me," Cam said, taking the water from me to hand it to Penelope. "We'll be right back," he told them, pulling me to the tiny bathroom and slamming the door shut behind us.

I laughed, almost feeling nervous as Cam's eyes roamed over my body. "Like what you see?" I asked.

He smiled, his fangs snagging on his lip. "I don't know where to start."

"Unzipping your pants might be a good place," I suggested, slipping my jeans off my hips. "I'm sure the rest will work itself out."

Making quick work of taking off his clothes, Cam stood naked in his demon form. "How do you want it, Mavis?"

Pulling him down to meet my mouth, I kissed him and murmured against his lips. "I want it with you, the real you, not your demon form."

In the blink of an eye, the Cameron DeSalle I'd met on that lonely highway in Utah was standing in front of me. "Better?"

"I'll be better when you have your cock between my legs," I told him.

Cam threaded his fingers in my hair, kissing me hard before sliding his hands down to cup my ass and pick me up. He groaned loudly as I moved my hand between us to lead him inside of my warmth, and I cried out as I sank down on him, pure, unadulterated pleasure shooting through my body like lightning.

"I love you, Mavis," he said as we moved together, both of us searching, reaching for that one perfect moment of ecstasy.

"I love you," I replied, eyes shut tight as a coil tightened deep within me and the first sweet sensations of orgasm flittered through me, making me tighten around his cock.

"Fuck!" Cam yelled, his eyes flickering between black and brown as he came closer to his own release.

"Take it," I whispered against his mouth, before licking it open and letting him breathe in the soul I'd been given. I cried out, the emotions I'd felt with his humanity amplifying to a crescendo and then stopping suddenly as if we were standing in the eye of a hurricane. I broke away, burying my face into his neck.

Roaring as the human feelings filtered through him, he turned me so that my back was against the wall and pounded into me until I was sore and trembling, my thighs slick. Both of us breathing heavily, we stared at each other, knowing what had just occurred between us was more than sex. It was the return of us—what we'd had before Severin had taken it all away.

"I have to admit," he said, smiling as he broke the silence. "I thought you'd want me in my demon form one last time."

I shook my head and softly kissed his lips. "I wanted the man I fell in love with, Cam. That's all I've ever wanted."

CHAPTER 13

*O*nce we were cleaned up and dressed, we walked out of the bathroom to meet Ray and Penelope. I was glad to see that they were sitting within a few feet of each other and talking, something I hadn't expected. I knew it would take a long, long time for him to convince her that she should forgive him, but this was definitely a start.

"Are you guys good?" Ray asked.

I held up the water bottle I'd picked up on the way out of the bathroom and froze it solid. "Yep."

"You?" he asked Cam.

Cam nodded, his honey-brown eyes alight with happiness instead of the emotionless black we'd become used to.

He smiled at us. "Good. I'll run upstairs and see where things are. Remember, there are still a few demon guards up there, in and out of the house. I don't want you to try to take them all on, on your own, Mavis. Severin can't escape in the chaos of another battle. He needs to be the first to die."

I nodded, steeling myself for what was to come. "Kill Severin first. Got it."

He turned to Penelope. "Are you ready? I can get you back to Havenwood Falls, then come back to help."

"Wait," Penelope said. "Are you sure we shouldn't stay? What if Severin notices that Mavis doesn't have a soul as soon as he sees her, and strikes first?"

"With what?" Cameron asked. "He can't defeat her. No demon can. The second she lets her power loose—well, you've seen what happens."

"It still sounds risky," she said, worry in her voice.

"I'll be fine," I assured her. "It will help me to know that you're safe and far away from what's going to happen here."

Reluctant to leave us, she hugged me and then Cameron. "Get home safely, guys. I'll be waiting."

Cameron tousled her hair and grinned, something he hadn't done in months. "We will, Penny. Now get out of this shithole and go home. Sam, Dean, and Castiel are waiting for you."

She grinned back at him and followed Rayonus up the stairs. "Love you, guys . . . even though your sex life completely grosses me out."

I laughed, shaking my head as we watched the door close behind them. "It's nice to see her smile again."

"Yes," he agreed. "Maybe now things can get back to normal."

"Or not," I hissed, as the light from the hallway above spilled onto the stairs.

Taking a fighting stance, we readied ourselves for whatever was about to happen and were surprised to see a gray-haired old woman with bright green eyes stroll down the stairs. "Severin wants to see you, Cameron," she said.

"Tell him to come down here himself," I told her. "He's not going anywhere."

She breathed out a very put-upon sigh. "Mavis, don't make this harder than it has to be on yourself. You don't want to piss me off. You can't win in a fight against me. Don't even bother."

I scoffed at the woman's presumption. "Wanna bet? Maybe you should worry about pissing me off."

She looked at Cameron. "Is she serious?"

Cameron looked from the woman to me and tried to relay something meaningful with his eyes. I just didn't know what that something was.

"Fine," the woman said, lifting her hands to her chest level, palms out. "I did try to warn you."

A little frightened now, I took a step back. "What are you doing?"

"Showing your smart mouth a lesson," she said, as a surge of power filled the room.

Putting my hands over my ears to stop the pressure in my head, I screamed and threw myself at her, only moving my hand away from my ear long enough to wrap one around her wrist and push my magic into her. The familiar pop shot through my chest, but the magic didn't stop the attack. In fact, it only seemed to make it worse.

Falling to my knees, the old woman cackled with laughter. "This will teach you to mess with the likes of me, demon!"

Just when I thought I couldn't take any more of the onslaught, Cam rushed to the other side of the room unnoticed and came back with a folding chair, which he promptly brought down on her head.

The pressure died down instantly, and I sagged to the ground with relief.

Cam was at my side in an instant. "Are you okay, darling? Talk to me. Are you hurt?"

I shook my head, though it made everything in the room seem to spin out of control. "I'm okay."

He held out a hand to help me up, and I took it, glad to have something in the room that wasn't spinning. "Do you need to sit down?"

"No," I said, trying to move away from the unconscious

woman. "We need to go. I don't think we should be here when she wakes up."

He glanced down at the woman's bleeding head. "No, definitely not. She will not appreciate the chair to the head."

"What is she?" I asked, intrigued by the green blood matted in her frizzled hair.

Cam shook his head. "Someone very powerful. I don't exactly know what, but she's been in line with my father for as long as I can remember."

I nodded and took a deep breath, careful to navigate the dark stairs as I climbed up with Cameron. We stopped at the top, and Cam peeked out into the hallway. "It's clear," he whispered.

"To the right," I reminded him, stopping to bolt the door behind us. "The other way leads back to the cell."

"Yes, it does, and that's exactly where you're going," said the voice I'd heard Ray say belonged to Felix.

Without thinking or stopping, I shot two spears of ice into the demon, pinning him to the wall through his shoulders. His screams echoed through the house, bringing two more guards running into the hallway.

"Fuck!" Cam yelled, grabbing me and yanking me the other way, back toward the cell we'd come from.

"No!" I said, resisting. "We can't go that way."

"What do you suggest then?" he asked, trying to shove me behind him.

"Move," I yelled, startling him into obeying me. "I've got this!"

Suddenly, in all the commotion and noise, I realized something that had never crossed my mind before. I was the Exitium Daemonium, but I was also an ice demon. I didn't know a ton of demons, but it was safe to say that I'd never met one with dual power. But somehow, I had it. What would happen if I combined my magic? Could I kill demons from afar with my ice?

Summoning my power to the forefront of my mind, I imagined

infusing it with the same spears I'd used on Felix, sending them spinning toward both guards running our direction. At first, nothing out of the ordinary seemed to happen, but as the ice stopped its forward motion and sank into the chests of the guards, they stopped and howled with pain before bursting into a fine mist of disintegrated demon.

Cam stared at me, dumbfounded. "Mavis, you can combine your magic?"

I nodded, making my way to Felix, who was still struggling to pry himself off the wall. When he saw me coming, he screamed in earnest, knowing what was happening next. Holding up my hand, I formed a long dagger and pushed my magic through it, bringing it down right into the center of his chest. His screams died instantly as his body shared the same fate as the others.

Cam seemed shaken for a moment, but then he rushed forward, keeping a hand on me as he led the way to the relative safety of outdoors.

We were almost to the front door when Severin walked into the room from what must have been the kitchen. The moment he saw us, he smiled and tsked as if we were naughty children who had snuck into the cookie jar.

"What do we have here?" he asked, a moment before he seemed to realize that the soul he'd given me was gone.

Moving quicker than we expected him to, he pulled a gun from his waistband and aimed it at his son, pulling the trigger twice before turning the gun on me and screaming, "You thought you could escape me? You thought I'd just let you go? I'm never letting you go. You will serve my every need for an eternity!"

Ignoring the gun he aimed at me, I fell down to my knees beside Cameron. I knew Severin wouldn't shoot me. He needed me. He had plans for me.

"Cameron," I said, shaking him when he didn't respond. "Cameron!"

Panic filled me as I saw the two bleeding bullet holes in his chest. He couldn't die like this. Not when we were so close. Not after everything we'd been through over the past six months. This couldn't be happening.

"Baby, please," I wailed, starting CPR. "Please, stay with me. I can't lose you."

"He's dead," Severin said coldly. "As he should be. He only had one job in his worthless life, to serve me, and he couldn't even do that right. He didn't deserve the breath I gave him when I impregnated his bitch of a mother."

Anger, white-hot and raging, filled me as his stinging words registered in my grief-addled brain. Worthless?

Lifting myself to my feet, I turned to Severin, my eyes not really seeing him. "Did you just call the love of my life worthless?"

Severin stepped back but didn't answer.

"Did you?" I screamed, no longer in my right mind.

"You're better off without him," he said, looking over Cameron with a sneer of distaste. "He was never what he could've been, should've been. He wasn't anything. Just a waste of oxygen."

Stunned, I stood there next to the body of the man I loved and stared at his father. I stared at the demon who had tortured him throughout his long life. I stared at the demon who had shot him and taken him away from me.

And then I snapped.

Throwing my arms wide, I shot two long shards of jagged ice into my grip, pushing my magic into every molecule of their makeup, and then I took a menacing step toward him. "I'm going to kill you, Severin. I'm going to see the light fade from your eyes. And I'm going to rejoice in the sound of your screams."

"Try it, ice demon," he said, inviting me forward. "You will rue the day you brought this suffering on yourself."

With a warrior's cry, I rushed forward, stabbing and slashing any part of him that I could reach. I could've done it without getting my hands dirty, but I wanted this. I needed this. It was my right to avenge my mate.

Severin laughed as the ice cut into him, not realizing the severity of his injuries until it was far too late. Finally looking down at himself, he saw his skin falling away in fragments. And then he screamed, and screamed, and screamed.

EPILOGUE

J never got to say thank you to Rayonus Rixa.

Sure, it was the demon's fault the three of us had gotten kidnapped, his fault Penelope had been distant since her dramatic return, and his fault Cameron had been shot, but even with all that taken into consideration, I couldn't deny that he'd given us the only opportunity we were likely ever to have to kill Severin DeSalle.

"Are you still pining over Rayonus?" Cam asked, kissing the top of my head before handing me a mug of chai tea.

I sighed and smiled, closing the journal I was writing in and throwing it to the coffee table. Hearing Cam's voice was a balm to my nerves and something I would never take for granted. He'd survived the gunshot wounds, but only just, and only because, underneath the human façade, he had the power of a demon running through his veins. It was fitting that the only thing that saved him was the one thing his father couldn't ever take away from him.

"I just wish he'd come back," I said, accepting the mug with a grateful smile.

Cam sighed and hugged me to his side. "I know, darling. I miss him, too."

For days upon days, after Cam healed, we searched and wondered and worried what had happened to Rayonus, but those days had turned into weeks, and though the hope we'd see him strolling into the apartment uninvited sometime soon was starting to feel like a far-fetched dream, we'd left all his things neatly stowed in the spare bedroom, on the chance that, one day, he'd come back for them . . . and for a devastated Penelope.

A knock at the door set my heart racing, as it always did since the incident. I ran to the door, hoping beyond hope that the black-and-blue-eyed demon would be standing there, giving us his trademark smirk, but just like all the times before, it was Penelope coming over to pass the time.

Tonight, I found her wearing one of Ray's favorite flannel shirts, a pair of leggings, and a weary smile. "Hi," she said. "It's almost time for *Supernatural*. Mind if I watch it over here?"

I pulled her inside and closed the door, happy she was doing something so ordinary. "Sure. Want some chai tea?"

She shrugged. "Sure. I'm probably going to die alone and be eaten by my twelve cats anyway. Why not start drinking old lady drinks now?"

Cam jumped up to make the tea before I had a chance to ask. He understood that Penelope was facing Ray's disappearance like she did any tough situation—with her trademark sarcasm and overreaction—but we were glad to suffer through it for her. We would do anything for her, especially after she'd planned our expedited wedding from top to bottom while I nursed Cam back to health.

"So, are you guys still getting married this weekend?" she asked.

Yes, we are," Cam said, handing her a steaming hot mug of tea. "And yes, you still have to come."

Cam sat back down next to me and squeezed my hand. Regardless of Ray seemingly vanishing into thin air, we weren't willing to wait any longer to be married. We'd been together through the worst months any couple could ever go through. There was no reason to put it off or prolong the engagement. We'd survived, and we had each other, and that was all that mattered.

"What do you think the odds are of me finding a hot demon guy at the reception?" Penelope asked as the front door opened unexpectedly.

I grinned and felt all the air leave the room as the newcomer came into sight. "Oh, I think the odds are pretty good."

We hope you enjoyed this story in the Havenwood Falls world featuring a variety of supernatural creatures. Havenwood Falls is a collaborative effort by multiple authors.

Books in the Havenwood Falls Sin & Silk series:

Taming the Beast by Nadirah Foxx
Plans Laid Bare by JD Nelson
Shift of Fate by Victoria Escobar
Stolen Wishes by Victoria Flynn
Damned Allure by Justine Winter
Savage Salvation by Kristie Cook
Dark Seduction by Michele G. Miller & R.K. Ryals
Soul Laid Bare by JD Nelson
Stray With Me by E.J. Fechenda
Chase the Flames by Desiree Lafawn
Flirting With Death by Nadirah Foxx

Also try the signature line, Havenwood Falls, the historical paranormal line, Legends of Havenwood Falls, and stories from the local supernatural college in Sun & Moon Academy.

Stay up to date at www.HavenwoodFalls.com

Subscribe to our reader group and receive free stories and more!

ABOUT THE AUTHOR

JD Nelson is a bestselling author of Fantasy Romance and Adult Paranormal Romance. An avid time-waster, JD enjoys watching TV and listening to audiobooks when she really should be writing.

JD loves to hear from her readers. You can contact her through her website, AuthorJDNelson.com, or on Facebook, where she spends an alarming amount of time chatting with her many author and reader friends, much to the dismay of her continually neglected manuscripts.

ACKNOWLEDGMENTS

I want to send a huge thank you out to the readers that wanted to murder me when I made *Plans Laid Bare* a cliffhanger. Without your restraint, this book would not be possible. XOXO

AN EXCERPT

~ A Havenwood Falls Sin & Silk Novella ~

HAVENWOOD FALLS

sin & silk

Stray with Me

E.J. FECHENDA

Stray With Me (A Havenwood Falls Sin & Silk Novella) by E.J. Fechenda

She's a rich witch with deep roots. He's a shifter biker with none. When a passionate fling becomes more, it also turns deadly.

Being a witch isn't all magic potions and conjuring up great outfits, especially when your last name is Augustine. As a descendant of a founding family of Havenwood Falls and granddaughter of a high priestess of their coven, she's been raised to adhere to certain expectations—suffocating and annoying expectations. Dating a biker is the exact opposite of those.

At first, it's an act of rebellion. Ryker "Crusher" Pride, enforcer in Swords of the Infernal Night motorcycle club, is like forbidden fruit. Where she has deep roots in town and a big family, Ryker is an orphan lion shifter who grew up on the streets. His family is the MC—"thugs and outlaws," according to her grandmother.

Ryker's brothers are convinced Harlow will break his heart and return to her side of the tracks. But what started as simple lust grows deeper. Ryker gives Harlow strength to stand up to her family. She inspires in him the desire to settle down and make a permanent home. When tragedy strikes, Harlow makes a rash decision out of love and quickly learns that her magic has consequences—deadly consequences that could cause Harlow to lose Ryker and be banished from Havenwood Falls.

STRAY WITH ME

BY E.J. FECHENDA

Harlow kept her pace and breathing even. Eyes focused on the road ahead. Sweat dripped down her back as she rounded the bend. Havenwood Falls stretched out before her as she ran down Blackstone Road. Creekwood Estates was to her right. Aspen trees, leaves already turning gold, added to the colorful landscape. Sunlight hit solar panels and twinkled brightly. To the left was the cemetery, and while she couldn't hear them, her sister Taylor said the dead often whispered to her when she passed by the hallowed grounds. Harlow's sister was a medium, though, so she wasn't surprised.

A car that Harlow recognized slowed to stop at the end of Stuart Street. She waved to Amanda George, and the young kindergarten teacher waved back before pulling out to make a left onto Blackstone Road, cutting off a motorcycle. Harlow inhaled sharply when she realized the motorcyclist didn't have time to slow down and would hit the car. Without thinking, Harlow snapped her fingers, and instantaneously, time came to a halt. The car and motorcycle paused, along with a bird flying overhead.

"Shit! You've really done it now," she scolded herself. Resigned to the fact that she had just used her magic in front of a human, she quickly proceeded to manipulate the car, so it completed the turn and was out of the way of the motorcycle. As soon as it was clear, she snapped her fingers, and time resumed.

Hoping Amanda, the human she had just used magic on, didn't notice, Harlow continued her run as if nothing had happened. Unfortunately, the man on the motorcycle did notice and pulled over to the side of the road, directly in front of her. She had heard about Ryker Pride, remembered when he arrived in Havenwood Falls a couple years ago. He was a lion shifter—a rarity in Colorado —and that had created some local gossip. The fact that he was hot and single had added to the gossip among her girlfriends.

Ryker had long, dirty-blond hair that was tangled from the wind. He removed his sunglasses, pinning her in place with smoldering blue-gray eyes. A thick layer of stubble blanketed his square jaw. He wore jeans and a long-sleeved flannel shirt that stretched over massive biceps. But the black leather vest he wore over his shirt revealed who he really was. The Swords of the Infernal Night, or SIN Motorcycle Club, was full of men her grandmother warned her about it. By the way Harlow's body responded just by standing within three feet of the giant piece of man candy, she knew her grandmother was right. This man needed to come with a warning label.

"Nice save back there, Country Club. I owe you one," Ryker said, his voice more like a sultry growl that caused her nipples to harden. When his gaze drifted down her body and he gave her a feral grin, followed by a wink, she knew he noticed. Of course, she was wearing a tight black running shirt over her sports bra and skintight leggings, leaving little to the imagination.

Swallowing hard, she crossed her arms over her chest and firmly met his gaze.

"Country Club?" she asked, narrowing her eyes.

His grin widened. "Just a nickname the boys have come up

with. Your pops is some big wig at the club and you work there, right?"

Harlow's eyes narrowed even further. "You sure know a lot about me for never having met before, and I already have a nickname? What's that all about?"

Sure, Havenwood Falls was a small town and her dad was the Director of Member Services at Creekwood Country Club, so he knew a lot of people, but that crowd generally didn't mix with bikers. Realizing she sounded judgmental, Harlow closed her eyes and took a deep breath to center herself. When she looked at the biker again, he had his hands in the air as if in surrender. He straddled his bike, a monster black and chrome machine that looked almost as dangerous as its rider.

"Hey, it's no big deal. My brothers and I take notice of all the beautiful single females in town. You're one of them."

Okay, so he's an ass—a hot ass, but an ass. Judgment totally earned, she thought to herself. Harlow was about ready to tell him off when her phone that was strapped to her right bicep started to ring. She glanced at the screen and saw her grandmother's name. Mathilde Augustine was the matriarch of the family, a leader in the Luna Coven, and she sat on the Court of the Sun and the Moon, which was the governing body of the supernatural community in Havenwood Falls. With a sinking sensation in her stomach, Harlow knew the use of her magic had triggered the wards that surrounded the town. Lately, Harlow's grandmother had been extra everything: nosy, controlling, and protective. Harlow didn't know what was going on, but she had heard whispers about an outside threat.

"Harlow, did you just use a little more magic than usual? Are you okay?" she asked when Harlow answered her phone.

"I'm fine, Grandma."

"Are you sure? Nothing unusual happened?"

"Nope, everything is fine."

"No witnesses?"

"Nope," Harlow lied, and she made eye contact with Ryker, whose eyebrows were raised. Based on his reaction Harlow knew he was able to hear the conversation. Shifters were known for their enhanced senses.

"Okay, dear. I was just worried." Harlow's heart softened, and any annoyance at her grandmother being overbearing vanished. She sounded more like a concerned grandmother than a critical leader. It had been a few months since Harlow got in trouble for using her magic in public, and she was relieved to not be on the receiving end of another lecture—or worse.

"No need to be. I'll see you soon. Bye."

She disconnected the call and reached up to tighten her ponytail, in preparation to start running again.

Ryker's gaze roved over her body before he said, "I can think of some other forms of exercise."

He winked at her and laughed when she rolled her eyes before turning away.

"You wish," she said over her shoulder and began to jog back the way she came.

"Wait!" he called out. "I was just fucking around. Want to go out for drinks or something? I owe you. I'd be a heap of road rash right about now if not for you."

"Nothing happened, okay? You didn't see anything." Harlow waved him off and kept running, knowing it was best to put distance between them.

The next morning, Harlow arrived at Coffee Haven to open. The sun was just beginning to rise, but it didn't hold much promise to beat back the cold. The weather in their box canyon town was unpredictable. A front had blown in overnight, ushering in temperatures low enough to make snow possible. The bell above the door chimed when she pushed it open, and she inhaled the fresh aroma of coffee brewing. The manager, Davis George, looked up from where he was placing a tray of scones in the display case. They said good morning, and Harlow jumped in on her opening chores. Davis became the manager more than a year ago, when he and his wife Amanda, the woman Harlow had stopped time for the day before, moved to town. Harlow and Davis had established a routine. Neither was usually talkative in the morning, so they worked well together. Except that morning, Davis had a story to tell, and it was one that made Harlow cringe.

"Amanda keeps going on and on about an experience she had yesterday. She claims it was divine intervention or something." Davis took off his dark-framed glasses and cleaned the lenses with the bottom of his apron.

"Really?" Harlow asked, wiping flour off the counter and pretending to be intrigued while ignoring the sinking feeling in her stomach.

"Yeah, she said you were there. She saw you running, and she waved at you, and the next minute, she said she almost collided with a motorcycle, but it was like time stopped or slowed down. She could see the stubble on his jaw, she was that close, but somehow, she avoided hitting him. Did you see it?"

Harlow chose her next words carefully. "I did see the close call, but I'd say it was just luck. I didn't see anything out of the ordinary."

"Good. I'll make sure to tell her that. She's been obsessing over it. I'm just glad she and Junior weren't in an accident."

"Same here." Harlow left the conversation at that, convinced she had nipped the situation in the bud.

There was a steady stream of business all day—customers eager to warm up with a hot coffee or cocoa. By closing time, Harlow had forgotten about the conversation. She and Davis left together, Davis locking the door behind them. They walked down the sidewalk, waving at Sedona, the owner of the bookstore next door, as she was in the front window setting up a new display. They walked several blocks, past the medical center, and Harlow split off to head up to her house. She hunched forward against the cold wind and burrowed her face in her scarf to keep her nose from freezing. Dusk was already descending; the days had noticeably begun to grow shorter.

She had just slipped her shoes off and hung up her jacket when her phone rang. It was her grandmother again.

"Grandma, what's up?" She walked down the short hallway into the kitchen.

"Imagine my surprise when Letitia Blackstone called me up just now with an interesting story."

"Okay . . . what story?" Harlow pulled out her rice cooker from the cabinet next to the refrigerator and set it on the counter.

"Amanda George was in an afternoon yoga class and couldn't stop talking about a miracle that happened."

Harlow groaned internally and hung her head. The beauty of living in a small town. There weren't any secrets, and of all people to overhear Amanda, it had to be Letitia Blackstone. She ran Yoga in the Vines at NamaStays Inn. She was also the retired matriarch of the Blackstone family, one of the founding families, like the Augustines. The two families shared a long history, and Letitia and her grandmother were friends. "The way Amanda described time stopping sounded awfully familiar, and it was right around the time the wards picked up a surge of your magic. Do you have anything to tell me?" Gone was the grandmother tone.

After breathing out a sigh, Harlow admitted she had used her magic to prevent an accident.

"You lied to me."

"Not really. I didn't think Amanda had noticed, so there wasn't anything to worry about. I'm sorry, Grandma. If I'd known, I would have wiped her memory, as I've been trained."

There was a long pause, and Harlow chewed on her lip. She hoped her grandmother didn't press further. If she revealed she had been distracted by a hot biker—well, that excuse would not fly.

Her grandmother breathed out a heavy sigh. "I have to report it to the Court, Harlow. It's my duty."

"But—"

"I can't show leniency because you're my granddaughter. It will call my leadership into question. I'm sorry. I came to your defense after the incident at the Dirty Knuckle, and it caused a stir. I'll let you know what they say."

Before Harlow could respond, her grandmother ended the call.

"Ugh!" she growled and tossed her phone onto the counter. The incident her grandmother referred to had happened over three months earlier, and she was still being punished for it—even though all she did was defend her friend, Shayna. Although, in hindsight, sending a guy flying across the bar for sticking his hand up her friend's skirt might have been a bit overkill, but she had zero tolerance for gropey fuckers, and the guy had been warned after he grabbed Harlow's ass earlier that night. Unfortunately for her, there was a room full of witnesses and a room full of cell phones, plus the guy was angry and wanted to press charges against her for assault. Considerable damage control had to be employed, and Harlow was called in front of the Court. Because of her grandmother, she had been dismissed with a stern warning. Somehow, she had a feeling she wasn't going to be so lucky this time.

Two days later, just before eight p.m. on Tuesday, Harlow parked her Mini Cooper in front of City Hall. She turned off the ignition and sat in her car, focusing on getting her breathing under control. Thoughts of her friend Aster ran through her mind. Aster and her sister, Reeve, had both been banished from Havenwood Falls for using their abilities in public. Fear rendered her immobile, her hands gripping the steering wheel tight. Aster and Reeve's situation was different; it was really, really public. Harlow hoped for a slap on the wrist. As much as she hated the suffocating confines of being an Augustine, she didn't want to be forced from where she was born and raised.

With a final deep exhale, she stepped out of her car and strode with false confidence down the walkway that led around back of the building, to the special entrance for the Court of the Sun and the Moon. Minutes later, Harlow sat at one of the two tables that faced the elevated dais where the members of the Court had convened. Addie Beaumont sat off to the side, taking minutes. A large mural depicting all of the supernatural species that resided in town provided a backdrop for the court members.

Elsmed Fairchild, the fae representative, spoke first, breaking the uncomfortable silence. His long silver hair was pulled back, drawing attention to his preternatural features: extremely pointy ears and a long, narrow face. So long his chin seemed to touch his chest. His penetrating icy blue gaze held Harlow captive. "Ms. Augustine. Your grandmother tells us you used a considerable amount of magic in public, in front of a human, is this correct?"

Harlow broke away from his gaze to look at her grandmother, who sat to the right of Elsmed. Her back was straight and hands clasped in front of her. Her expression didn't betray any emotion.

"That's correct. There would have been a terrible accident," Harlow started to plead her case, but was cut off by Lawrence Mills. His sharp voice silenced her.

"This is your second offense, is it not? You received a pass the last time." He cast a severe glance at Harlow's grandmother. Harlow swallowed hard.

"Lawrence, let the girl speak," Sandra Beaumont, Addie's grandmother, said. Mr. Mills huffed and leaned back in his chair, crossing his arms over his chest. "Tell us what happened, Harlow."

Harlow relayed the brief incident, making sure to emphasize that Amanda George hadn't seemed aware that anything unusual had occurred.

"Amanda George, the kindergarten teacher?" Mayor Barbie Stuart spoke up. The mayor was the only human who sat on the Court. It made sense that all species, including humans, had representation. With her height and large build, though, the mayor could have been a supe. Perhaps some giant blood ran in her genes. Add in a sky-high bouffant of cotton-candy-pink hair, and she certainly didn't look like a typical politician.

"Yes, and her child was in the car. When I knew an accident was imminent, I reacted. It was a knee-jerk reaction and not an intentional disregard of the law."

"Hmph," Lawrence huffed again.

"She speaks the truth," Elsmed said, after Harlow felt his presence inside her head probing her thoughts. A sensation she had experienced once before and would never get used to—like the tip of a feather was being dragged across her brain.

"Sounds like your granddaughter needs better control over her reactions, Mathilde," Lawrence said to Harlow's grandmother. "And a reminder of the Luna Coven's role: to use magic to cover up mishaps, especially when a human is exposed—not to create a problem."

"Harlow does understand the coven's role. Remember when she covered up after Paisley Underwood healed that human in public? However, I agree she needs to work on her impulsiveness. The coven will address that. I will see to it."

Harlow ground her molars together to keep her mouth shut. Her grandmother, a high priestess of the Luna Coven, had been trying to pull her into coven business more and more. Harlow preferred to stay on the periphery and do her own thing, but her mishap had just given her grandmother leverage.

"The younger generations have zero respect anymore and lack discipline. I propose we start implementing harsher punishments, or they're going to continue to disregard the law. An example must be made! We have more pressing issues at hand, and if people can't follow the law, then I say we be done with them!" Lawrence glowered from under his bushy eyebrows. He opened his mouth to say something else but he was interrupted.

"You mean my generation, Lawrence?" Michaela Petran chided and rolled her eyes. "Because of these issues you mention, we need every capable witch, which Harlow very much is. I propose she does receive further training, though. I believe that would make everyone happy, Lawrence?" The moroi vampire dipped her head in deference to the elder frost dragon shifter. Harlow silently cheered, thankful for Michaela's support. She was also curious about the issues they were referring to that would require every capable witch. What exactly was going on?

"I propose the three-strike rule should apply. One more incident will be the third strike and grounds for banishment," Roman Bishop added in a bored tone. He straightened the sleeves of his suit jacket and brushed at the fabric as if it were covered in dust. Harlow couldn't see any imperfection, and that was Roman, always perfectly dressed and exuding confidence.

"That seems reasonable. Shall we put it to a vote?" Elsmed motioned. There were murmurs of agreement, and when he called for everyone in favor to say aye, Harlow waited, scarcely breathing, for the Court to determine her fate.

A sigh of relief rushed out of her lungs when all but one member voted in favor. She wasn't surprised Lawrence Mills opposed. She'd heard he was a stickler for the rules and old school. Before she could leave, Harlow had to agree to training, and Mathilde would oversee her progress. Another term of the agreement was that if Harlow used her magic in the presence of a human again, without ensuring memories were altered to cover up the incident, she could face immediate banishment.

After that, she was free to go, and she left quickly, rushing up the stairs, pushing open the door, and stepping out into the night. The cool, fresh air was a jarring transition from the oppressive

Court's chambers, and she paused to take a few deep breaths. When she reached the end of the walkway and started to approach her car, she was surprised to see someone waiting for her. Ryker sat astride his bike, which was parked next to her Mini. He was leaning forward, his arms resting on tall handlebars with his large hands draping over top. He was facing her, and she felt the weight of his gaze. She faltered and came to a stop in front of her car. He was parked on the left, and she'd have to pass him to get to the driver's side door.

"What are you doing here?" she asked.

"I happened to be driving by and saw you walking in. Does this have anything to do with the other day? Are you good?"

"Oh." Surprised at his concern, she let her guard down and relaxed. Her shoulders seemed to melt away from her ears, and she didn't realize how tense she had been. "I'm okay. Thanks for checking in."

At that moment she heard her grandmother approaching, recognizing her voice by the almost Southern drawl. Harlow looked over her shoulder to see her grandmother walking with Lawrence Mills. Wanting to avoid her, Harlow rushed over to her door. Just as she had her hand on the handle, her grandmother called out.

"Harlow, I need to speak with you!"

"Fuck," she muttered under her breath, and dipped her head forward, causing a cascade of dark waves to shield her face.

"You can hop on the back of my bike and escape," a deep voice growled from behind her. Harlow let out a sigh. Releasing the door handle, she turned to face Ryker.

"Tempting, but my grandmother kind of has me by the balls right now. I need to hear her out."

Ryker chuckled and shook his head. "Quite the mouth you have there, Country Club." He smirked.

"Sorry, did I offend the big bad biker? I didn't realize you were so sensitive."

Another chuckle rumbled from his barrel chest. "Not at all. I like it."

A throat being cleared interrupted their banter, and Harlow stifled a groan as she looked over at her grandmother who was standing at the curb's edge, eyes darting between her and Ryker. She pursed her lips.

"Harlow, I need to speak to you. Alone." Mathilde directed this toward Ryker, dismissing him with a single word.

"Whatever," Ryker growled and fired up his bike. He backed out of the spot and dipped his head in Harlow's direction. "See ya 'round, Country Club," he called before roaring off, the rumble of his pipes vibrating through her.

Harlow watched him go, enjoying the way his arm muscles bunched as he controlled his motorcycle, instantly regretting that she didn't take him up on the offer of escaping with him.

"Really, Harlow, a SIN member? Since when did you start associating with them? I don't approve and don't think your father will, either."

"Grandma, I don't hang out with SIN. I just met that guy when I saved his ass."

"Well, good. You're an Augustine, and we don't socialize with thugs and outlaws."

Harlow shook her head and pressed her lips together to keep from smirking. Roman Bishop and his brothers had a legendary reputation of conducting business that wasn't exactly on the up and up, and yet Roman sat on the Court. The fact that he was also from one of the town's founding families, wore fancy suits, and lived in Havenwood Heights helped people see past any indiscretions.

"What did you need to talk to me about?" she asked, eager to salvage the rest of her night.

"Are you scheduled to work at the country club Saturday night?"

"No. I'm working during the day at Coffee Haven. Shayna and

I are going to grab drinks somewhere after her shift at the medical center. Why?"

"Cancel. Saturday you start your lessons with me, and I'm having a dinner party after. Your attendance is mandatory." Her grandmother spun and started to walk away while Harlow stood there with her mouth hanging open in disbelief. She felt like she was twelve again and being reprimanded. "Be at my house by four and bring something nice to change into. Don't be late!" Her grandmother called over her shoulder and waved her hand in the air, causing the giant moonstone ring she always wore to flash. Whether it was night or day, the ring seemed to attract any light. Mathilde's long skirt billowed as she walked down the sidewalk.

"Unbelievable. I'm a grown ass witch and don't need lessons," Harlow muttered to herself as she slid into her car and turned on the engine, cranking the heat.

The next day Harlow wasn't working at either of her jobs, and she started the morning off with a latte and some retail therapy.

Harlow breathed in deep, inhaling the familiar, tantalizing smells of fresh coffee and baked pastries. There was always good energy in Coffee Haven, and that's why she liked working there. Strategically placed crystals, live plants, and colorful artwork on the walls, from local artists, kept the atmosphere positive. Her boss, Willow Fairchild, was behind the marble counter. Willow's long silvery-blond hair—similar to her great-grandfather Elsmed's hair and a common fae trait—was pulled back in a ponytail, and her black apron was dusted with flour. She was mixing batter in a large red bowl.

"Hey, what are you doing here on your day off?" she asked.

"I need my fix," Harlow said with a grin and walked around behind the counter to make herself a latte, expertly working the espresso machine. Right before she steamed the milk, she added a drop of vanilla in to sweeten it a little. As soon as it was ready,

Harlow took a sip, and even though she almost scalded her tongue, she groaned with pleasure.

"Wow. Just one sip and your mood shifted. Your love for coffee is real," Willow joked, as she poured the batter she had been mixing into muffin tins. Willow was an empath and could pick up moods and energy a person was emitting. "Rough day?"

"You could say that."

"Want to talk about it?"

Harlow looked around the shop at the few customers seated at tables throughout. It was between the early morning and lunch rushes, so quieter than usual. Leaning in closer to Willow and keeping her voice down, she filled her boss in on everything that had happened and recounted her meeting with the Court. She hadn't said anything to Willow earlier, or to anyone else, because she didn't want anyone to worry—or fight her battles for her. Willow would have gone to Elsmed.

"Davis told me about Amanda's experience, but it sounds like she's already moved on. Wait, back up. Who is Ryker?"

"He's the biker Amanda would have hit."

"He made an impression on you," Willow said with a sly smile and a wink, her turquoise blue eyes sparkling. The timer buzzed on the oven. She put oven mitts on before pulling a tray of steaming hot muffins out and setting it on the counter to cool.

"Not really. He's kind of an ass. A real bro type. All muscle and cockiness."

Willow snorted and shook her head as she untied her apron and tossed it in the hamper under the counter. "Your words don't match with what I'm sensing. Your aura lights up like a fireworks display whenever you mention him. You're definitely attracted to him."

"Pft. I am not," Harlow sputtered. Visions of Ryker's muscular body filled her mind, causing a flush to wash over her.

"Uh huh. Sure!" Willow teased. "You can't fool me. I say go for it. Didn't you just tell me last week that you needed to end your dry streak? Bad boys have an appeal. Go scratch that itch, girl!"

Harlow was still laughing at her boss when she left Coffee Haven and went next door to check out Callie's Consignments. If she had to suffer through one of her grandmother's hoity toity dinner parties, she was going to splurge on a new outfit for the occasion. Stepping inside the boutique was like stepping back in time. Callie specialized in vintage. One wall was lined with heavily beaded gowns that sparkled like jewels in the sun pouring in from the large storefront window. Classic denim and leather items that were just as trendy now as they were in the fifties caught her attention, particularly a leather vest that reminded her of a biker who was occupying too much space in her thoughts. She lifted the hanger off the rack and subtly brought the vest to her nose, taking a deep sniff. The rich oily scent seemed almost exotic and forbidden to her, but there wasn't anything special about it—it was just a leather vest.

"Did you just smell that?" Callie asked from directly behind Harlow, making her jump. She had been so fixated she hadn't heard the store owner approach.

"I like the smell of leather," she responded, a little defensively.

"Your newfound love of leather smell doesn't have anything to do with Ryker, does it? I saw you two talking last night." Callie gestured with her head in the direction of City Hall, her long dark brown hair shifting with the movement.

"You know Ryker?"

Callie shrugged. "I know of him. I think he's delivered packages to Ronan. I didn't realize you were friends with him?"

The question hung in the air unanswered as Harlow processed the information. Callie and Ronan were an on-again, off-again couple and had lately been on-again. Ronan Bishop was one of Roman's younger brothers, and Harlow had heard through the coven grapevine that if you needed to procure something through untraceable channels, Ronan was the guy you went to. She shouldn't have been surprised that Ryker and Ronan knew each other, but she was, and a little disappointed.

"I don't know him. We just met the other day. Anyway, I'm here about an outfit." Harlow changed the subject, and soon she and Callie were going through the racks. When she left the store over an hour later, she had a ruby-red dress in one hand and a pair of black leather boots with four-inch spiked heels in the other. They were an impulse buy after she imagined riding on the back of Ryker's bike, her arms wrapped around his barrel chest and her thighs pressed against his.

It wasn't going to happen. It couldn't. Her grandmother would have a stroke. But the idea of breaking free of her familial obligations, of having a fling with a bad boy was appealing—not that she'd ever act on it, especially since she now had to be on her best behavior. At least with the boots she could fantasize.

Purchase *Stray With Me* where books are sold.